I0674576

KAWANGA

Kawanga, an obscure outback town west of Sydney, Australia, is the focal point of an intercontinental quest for a missing, ancient document. The search party includes: ex-martial artist Donald Brant; French femme fatale Camille; British detective Sergeant Bonnington; as well as Harley, a hardened seaman, and his motley crew of money-hungry henchmen. His Majesty's servant, Lord Conley, into whose care the paper was entrusted, must retrieve it before it falls into the wrong hands. Catastrophic consequences are sure to follow otherwise, since this document would, if revealed publicly, deed present-day Sydney back to the Aborigines!

This fast-paced mystery is a nonstop adventure filled with intrigue, romance, action, and heart-pounding suspense. For everyone involved, all roads lead to— Kawanga!

Borgo Press Books by JACK HALLIDAY

Kawanga: A Mystery Novel
Swan Song and Other Mystery Stories

KAWANGA

A MYSTERY NOVEL

JACK HALLIDAY

THE BORGO PRESS

MMXII

KAWANGA

Copyright © 1988, 2012 by Jack Halliday
First published in different form in a 1988 limited edition.

FIRST BORGO PRESS EDITION

Published by Wildside Press LLC

www.wildsidebooks.com

DEDICATION

For Richard Norton,
Martial artist, action film star, friend.

CONTENTS

CHAPTER ONE

Heat.

Blinding, blistering, blazing heat.

How had he gotten here?

Where was he, anyway?

And why this incredible heat?

His shirt was a drenched beach towel. Sweat stung the creases of his neck as he strained to look up from the sand on which he sprawled, face down.

He winced and gasped as the sun seared his eyes for the split second he took to look directly in front of him. Ninety-three million miles were reduced to a few hundred yards; the white globe was sucking the life from him as it hung suspended in a cloudless sky on the horizon.

His face fell back onto his folded arms; he lapsed into unconsciousness...again.

* * * * * * *

The ceiling fan turned slowly, rhythmically, one with the heartbeats of the men gathered around the dusty, wooden table.

"He's gone; finished; history," Harley muttered. He spat the words out through pursed lips surrounded by a week's growth of beard. He leaned back in his chair, contented. He folded his arms over his pot belly and with a pompous smile nodded as if to punctuate his "verdict." He straightened his musty excuse for a hat and waited for the others to reply.

Tom shifted in his seat. A drop of perspiration ran down his spine, chilling him, causing the hairs on his sunburned forearms to stand up.

"I still don't understand," Tom said. His brow furrowed as he vocalized his uneasiness. "What if he left it...with someone...the girl; or what if the old man got a hold of it?"

"What if the old man has it; what if the old man has it?" he said, his anxiety becoming panic.

Harley rocked forward on his chair, his gnarled elbows landing with a thud on the table. The bartender looked up from his glass-drying, his eyes widening with interest.

The rough seaman strained closer, squinted into the eyes of the men across from him and whispered, "I said he's done. It's all finished, and he's not coming back and no one has it and it's over!" He slapped his pudgy palms on the table, grabbed his drink and sent the whiskey down his throat. He patted his stomach as the gentle warmth began to radiate through him. He leaned back in his chair once again and surveyed his nervous comrades.

Tom shook his head, unconvinced.

"Okay. What about you two? Are you sure it's so, 'over?'"

The boys looked at each other, then Harley, then Tom, sheepishly, wishing for all their lives the whole thing had never happened.

"Sure...sure it's over," Jim said. "Me and Toby...why, we're gonna relax now. "Ain't that right, Toby?" he said, a half-smile creeping over his face.

"Damn right. S'far as we're concerned, we did our part; we settled it; and it's all over. We're outta here," he sighed, trying to speak a confidence he lacked. The boys heartbeats were definitely out of step with the slow-turning ceiling fan now.

Harley smiled.

"Well...then...what's left?"

"Nothing," Tom mumbled. "Nothing at all." He looked out the window at the desert expanse.

Night would fall soon. The barren terrain would offer a

different type of cruelty: cold.

His thoughts were a million miles from the dingy bar.

"Nothing at all," he muttered.

CHAPTER TWO

Sydney was never really cold. Still, the air had a slight chill, nature's token winter weather for an eastern metropolis of the land at the bottom of the globe.

Harriet quickly made her way around the corner and nearly ran up Henley Street to the Post Office. She glanced at her watch: 4:50 p.m. She would make it. Once inside, her cold fingers were uncooperative as she fumbled the key into the box. She whisked the envelope into her purse and was back in her car by five o'clock.

She had never really gotten used to how it just 'dropped dark' in Australia. Twilight was illegal; day and night alternated with the ease of tag-team wrestlers. She breathed in a large lung-full of air and sighed it out again. "Sydney, you're beautiful!" she thought. She smiled as she drove towards the crimson horizon, the opera house looking on, as if appreciating her assessment of this busy city in the "Lucky Country."

Meanwhile, her future lay in a manila envelope in her purse on the seat beside her. One edge poked out between the shoulder straps, attempting an inarticulate conversation, a warning, really. Almost an insistence that this young, attractive brunette no longer take for granted her surroundings or her affluence, or...her life.

CHAPTER THREE

"Don't trifle with me, Bonnington. I have no use for triflers, no use at all."

Bonnington's face remained blank. It displayed no trace of his thoughts.

"Fat, pompous sow," he thought. "Overbearing, inconsiderate, egotistical pig!"

"I want the 'property' returned...immediately!

"No more delays; no more excuses; no more stalling; just results, NOW!"

Conley bellowed and his voice boomed back and forth from the shiny, marble floor to the ornate ceiling. He had not seen his feet in years, and at six foot five, he was a relative of the biblical Goliath. Indeed, the flowing beard and opulent clothing fitted him for a role in any historical epic. His stomach swayed as he leaned over his polished mahogany desk. His knuckles were white under the weight. He lowered his voice as he looked into the eyes of this former police detective. He chose his words carefully, as though each one had a price, in gold.

"I don't care if you never sleep again. I don't care what you eat, or if you eat. I'm not in the slightest interested in you.

I want it back, NOW!"

"Ungrateful louse," Bonnington responded, inaudibly.

"I understand, Mr. Conley," Bonnington replied, still devoid of any visible emotion.

"I'm doing all that I can," he assured his burly employer.

"Rome wasn't built in a day, you know," he chuckled,

nervousness surfacing for the first time.

"I'm not interested in bloody Rome! I'm not paying you to spout clichés! Get out and get it back and get it back NOW!"

He backed out of the office. The huge bookcases built into the walls on either side seemed to sway towards each other in obeisance to the wealthy man in front of the bay window.

The detective pulled the door towards him and left Conley a silhouette, the afternoon sun behind him.

CHAPTER FOUR

Of all the invisible commodities of life, what he needed most now was understanding. But where to find it? Who could understand? The whole experience was so bizarre, so surrealistic that he often wondered himself if it had all really happened. How do you get involved in situations totally out of character for you? What is it in us that makes us go beyond the limits of our morality into the undiscovered depths of our unconsciousness?

Tom was definitely not convinced that the whole business was over, Harley's bravado notwithstanding. No, there was something wrong, terribly wrong, so wrong that it nagged at him like a terrier at a trouser cuff. He couldn't shake it.

And Harriet. Could he just let the chips fall with her? Could he just dismiss her and their relationship with Harley's ease?

He put one foot on the bridge railing. The rail was cold under his fingers as he braced himself against the wind. The Pittsburgh sky-line sparkled, one neon maze in the October night. He looked to the left at the traffic pouring into town. He stood there, lost in thoughts of his adolescence. Less than a mile away was the theater he had worked at in high school. He breathed deeply and exhaled twenty years of memories, dates, work, shopping and...security. The simple experience of security.

Where had this "normalcy" gone; and where had the madness begun?

CHAPTER FIVE

C.J. strode down the hall, enjoying the smell of the newly laid carpet and the feel of it under his loafers. Sunlight flooded the hallway from the window directly in front of him. He stopped, just outside of the copy room, half-sat on the marble ledge. Twenty stories below, twenty thousand or more office workers scampered to their destinations: ants in a corporate maze. He felt deliciously separated from them; today he was a god surveying trapped humanity from a twenty-story heaven. The feeling was...exhilaration. The door opened, jerking his eyes and attention from the view outside to the one inside. His "escape" from monotony was less than a dozen feet away; today she was wearing black, all black except for the white pearl necklace gently hugging her throat.

"I swear I can never get this thing to work!"

She slammed the copier lid down, cocked one hip and rolled her eyes for an invisible audience.

She wasn't really his "type." She was tall, almost as tall as he. And then her wide-set eyes, dished face and dark hair made her appear almost oriental. If she possessed an hour glass figure, time was passing quickly. She was definitely not the large-breasted woman he had thought of "falling for." That was it, wasn't it? He had fallen for her; just like one of those "made-for-TV" movies. He was living a short story.

"Rita," he laughed.

"Are you still dueling with that poor unarmed metal soldier?"

"C.J.!" she yelled. "Pleeez get this thing working. I swear it does this to me on purpose!" She stood there, papers folded in her right hand, her knuckles braced on that cocked right hip.

"Definitely man's work," C.J. laughed. He stood over the machine, watching the copies come out one-by-one, wishing there were a thousand more waiting.

She was separated; he was married. Something "new" should be invented for the feeling that passed between them. It was the copy machine, then coffee breaks in the employees' lunchroom, most recently a dinner...to sort out that G.E. mix-up. He looked up from the machine into her clear, green eyes. He really was feeling his own pulse throbbing against his collar. She smiled, folding her arms in front of her. She looked at him with...understanding, almost like an older sister, innocent but aware.

"This is going to be trouble," he sighed.

She nodded, "I know."

CHAPTER SIX

Only one more inch.

Maybe an inch and a half. He reached down, past his guts, for the rest of his life's allotment of adrenaline and strained in one last attempt to cast his fingers toward the rim above him. The unfinished metal tore his skin as he clamped one, then the other hand over the edge of the tube into which he'd been dumped. He was human garbage to them. Time and exposure would finish what fists and feet had left undone.

Tom looked at his watch. The cracked crystal magnified: 7:30 p.m. Night had just fallen when he'd grabbed the cab to the office. He'd only been a few minutes on the bridge; he hadn't eaten supper. How long had he been unconscious? How far away were they by now?

He was up, out of the garbage chute now, slapping the dust from his trouser legs. One small, naked light bulb lit the hallway. It was cold and still and quiet, the opposite of his heartbeat.

He lunged up the metal stairs, grabbed the rail and swung himself onto the landing. The heavy door clanged shut behind him as he stood outside in the alley. He slumped back against the cold, red brick, strands of his hair catching on the rough mortar. He hugged himself, trying to deaden the sickening, dull ache in his ribs. The city was oblivious to either his pain or his plight. Tires screeched on wet asphalt.

CHAPTER SEVEN

C.J. sauntered over to the sink, filled a glass with water, gulped it and squinted out the window.

"I think we're involved," he called over his shoulder, smiling, waiting for her reply.

"Yeah; that's what they call it in the movies," Rita hollered in from the living room.

"So what are we supposed to do now? Get married?" she laughed.

"Beats me black and blue" he said, turning to face her. He leaned against the sink, the enamel creasing his elbows.

"It's sure going to be strange at work now. I can't even imagine working together; can you?"

"Let's don't even think about work," Rita mused, tossing her head back against the couch cushion, peering down her nose at him, a smile playing at the corner of her mouth.

"O.K, let's don't," he replied.

* * * * * * *

It wasn't that Bonnington was inept, not in the slightest. On the contrary, he was a veteran policeman with thirty years of experience. He'd seen a lot; experienced a lot. He'd drunk enough "stake-out" tea to float an ocean liner. No question, dues had been paid, beats walked, respect earned, by the proverbial, "blood, sweat and tears."

This case was just different.

For one thing, he didn't know—not actually—what he was looking for. A high ranking British official had simply hired him on the basis of his record. He was to retrieve a piece of "property," presumably a document of some kind, which had very possibly made its way to Australia.

No, it hadn't been wise to drink away most of his life's earnings and "piss it away" at a dozen pubs in London's east end. But that was behind him now; now he had to succeed—this once—and earn the nest egg his indulgence had hatched prematurely.

His mind raced in time with the train as it made its way to Heathrow. How had his career come to depend on this: a "pre-retirement send-off," an anticlimactic "one for the road?"

He closed his eyes, let his head slump against the cool window pane. The lights striking his closed lids merged with a tired reverie of the trip he was embarking upon. A trip to what was once an English convict's last stop, what was now, instead, an island paradise.

CHAPTER EIGHT

The house was dark as Harriet pulled into the driveway. She got out of the car, swung the door closed, caught it, reached back in and scooped up her purse, balancing it with her keys in her right hand; the envelope tumbled out as she re-closed the car door. It lay on the wet gravel in front of her, a gem in a rustic setting. Harriet bent over to retrieve it and dropped her keys. She grunted and crouched down, grabbed all of her things and unlocked the door. She flicked the light switch with her elbow.

World War Three had been fought in the living room of No. 10, Lindon St.

She gasped, dropped her purse, and her keys, slumped into the sofa, rested her heels on the hardwood floor.

The envelope lay in front of the fireplace, center stage.

"What on earth is happening to me?" she asked herself in the quiet of the Sydney evening.

The envelope was magnetic; her eyes were fastened to it now. It seemed almost to taunt her, to dare her to open it and further complicate her life, to add intrigue to extra-marital affair. Her mind reeled. She thought of Tom, of the intrusion of "romance" into her life, and at "her age." She folded her arms, clutched herself, feeling the pain of her infidelity. "Money, marriage, madness!" she thought as she brooded over her relationship with Tom. And he was gone, in America. "And you're here, alone," she thought, lashing herself with her words.

"What was in that envelope?"

She slid off the sofa and sat, Indian-style on the bare floor.

She picked up the envelope, turned it over, ran her long, ruby thumbnail along its edge, breaking the glue and tape sealing it. The "precious cargo" was a nearly blank sheet of typing paper, blank except for one lone word in the center of the page:

Kawanga.

CHAPTER NINE

Donald Brant was in one helluva mess.

He lay there, thinking about the plush surroundings of the hotel room back in Sydney. How he longed for a shower, some food, a return to civilization. He was sure he hadn't been abandoned here more than a day and a half. His athletic background assured him of survival without water for three days, without sleep for four, and a month or more without food.

He was all right.

It took all the strength he could muster, but he did it. He pushed and strained and finally flipped himself over onto his back. He guessed it was after six o'clock. The sky above was a deep purple. He lay in the sand trying to get his bearings. He sat up slowly, resting most of his weight on his elbows, surveying the situation. The air was clear, the night quiet, a few faint stars watched overhead. He scanned the horizon and then eased himself up onto his feet. He swayed, regained his balance and began the slow trek toward town.

A mirage at night?

The sound of a Jeep engine approached him from a distance like a bullet. The vehicle spun in front of him spraying him with sand. Toby, one of Harley's men, sat there, poker-faced, the engine idling roughly. The only sound was Toby's voice, nasal, unemotional. He ordered, "Get in."

Brant barked, "Get in? First you and the others leave me here to die and now you expect me to give you another crack at it?"

"Get in, now! Quick, before Harley and Jim get wise to

this, Mate. Look, we didn't know nothin' 'bout no killings. The money...that's all we're about, Jim and me. Just the money, Sport; now get in!"

Brant swung himself up into the Jeep and the pair sped off, back to the town, back to Kawanga.

* * * * * * *

The Jeep's lights illuminated the hotel sign reading "Dew Drop Inn." Toby reached in the back and tossed a duffel bag at Brant who stood, hands on his hips, in front of the hotel door. He caught it, letting it dangle from his hand. Two strange bedfellows stared at each other in the moonlight.

"Look, Brant, as far as Harley and the others are concerned, you're dead...or as good as. They're not even going to look for your corpse. You just get outta here. First thing tomorrow get to Adelaide...get to Timbuktu for all I care. Get a few thousand miles between here and you and you're apples, Mate."

Brant shook his head in incredulity. "Why are you doing this?"

"I done told you, Sport, killing's not in me plans; never was. That bastard, Harley, crazy sonuvabitch, Mate. Crazy as a loon he is. Me and Jim? We're off to the west in a few. Tom's back in the States already the way I get it. Man, I tell you, this whole thing's over."

Brant's brows furrowed. "What do you mean, 'over'?"

"Take my advice: get outta here. Stay one helluva long distance from Harley. Stay clear of *him* and she'll be sweet, Mate. Oh...and I reckon you could say you owe me one."

Toby sneered a parting grin at Brant and shot away, leaving a cloud of dust in his wake. Brant stood still, hands on his hips, still shaking his head in disbelief. To himself, he sighed, "What the hell?"

CHAPTER TEN

Conley poured himself another glass of apricot sherry. He let the glass just gently touch his lips while he inhaled the fruity aroma. The sun was just setting outside his Yorkshire home. He slid his chair back from his desk, swiveling it around to face the window. He licked his lips and surveyed the lush green acreage belonging to his mansion. Everything could remain intact, everything. His standing, his influence, his power, his wealth; he could keep it all. Her Majesty's public servant had hired an efficient "eraser" to remove even the memory of this misfortune. As he mused along these lines, Anderson, his butler, entered the office. "Any word from Bonnington, Sir?" he asked.

Conley swiveled his chair back to his desk, ran his fingers back and forth against the cool leather chair arm as he faced Anderson. "Not yet, but I'm satisfied he has the situation well in hand. I'm quite sure the document will be returned by the end of the month...perhaps sooner. Actually, I believe Mr. Bonnington has all the makings of quite an effective 'cleaner.'"

Anderson countered, "And the American woman?"

Conley inspected his study with a regal look. He sat here as king, never mind that "technical Sovereign's" home in London. He replied, "You've been with me for a long time. My 'relationship' with Rita is a memory...a slight libidinous excess."

Anderson blushed, replying, "Yes, Sir. I only meant...."

"Meant what?" Conley interrupted. That her majesty would somehow discover and discipline me?"

Anderson replied, "I meant no impertinence, Sir."

Conley steepled his fingers to his lips and turned his back on the butler to face the window, speaking with his back to him. "I'm more concerned with my *wife's* whereabouts. Another one of Camille's shenanigans might prove to be a political embarrassment to me."

"I'm sure you'll hear from her soon."

Conley swiveled his chair back to face him. "Yes, I'm certain I will. She's probably tied up with another good looking low-life. No matter; when the excitement runs down, she'll do what she's always done: return to 'Daddy'."

Anderson replied, reassuringly, "I have no doubt, Sir."

"Then, that will be all for now."

Anderson bowed as he replied, "As you wish."

With that, the burly sovereign turned again to face the window.

CHAPTER ELEVEN

It seemed like they had been together forever. Maybe it was the fact that she was older, maybe that she was more mature somehow. The past few weeks seemed to have blended into one tangled ball of physical and emotional love of a certain sort. He had divorced Carla emotionally years ago, now he was acting on the fact. Maybe his and Rita's relationship would "upset the cosmos"; she was the one who should have gotten away.

The restaurant was quiet; the only sounds were the quiet conversations of lovers and the faint kitchen sounds of Chinese food preparation. C.J. was devouring "Hong Kong chicken." Everywhere they went the surroundings were a movie set. Their romance was picture-perfect.

'Seriously, C.J.; will we get married?" asked Rita, stabbing the chow mein with her fork.

'Honey, I really don't know. I'm sure not afraid of marriage... or commitments: God, I stuck it out with Carla for nearly eight years."

"It's just that, well, maybe I need the sense of security; that we're real, all of this. I've never experienced this," Rita continued. "Definitely not while I was in England. And now that I'm back in the States permanently, well, maybe it's time for me to do something normal, like marriage."

"What did happen, I mean in England?" C.J. asked. His curiosity demanded that he pry. He honestly wanted to possess every part of her: past, present and future.

"I've told you already, C.J. I just did a relatively unsuccessful stint as an assistant at the American consulate. I got bored; I came home." She looked down at her plate, avoiding his searching eyes.

"That's it...no...men?" C.J. was as uncomfortable asking as she was answering.

"One...one man," she whispered, looking away to the kitchen. She looked back at him, stared sternly into his eyes. "It only lasted about a month; then it was over." She burst into a smile. "And he was a lord or something. Can you believe it, C.J.? Me, with a member of 'royalty?'"

He coughed, trying to disguise the hot flame of jealousy flashing through his stomach. "Wow, that is crazy," he laughed. "You and a lord, of all things; crazy." His smile faded.

CHAPTER TWELVE

"Donald Brant, I still hate you!"

Harriet sat there in the middle of the floor, holding the paper in her hand, watching movies in her mind of her ex-husband's "wilderness wanderings."

"What's in Kawanga, for God's sake?"

She reached into the storehouse of her thoughts, straining her memory for even a small bit of input related to the outback town.

"Kawanga," she repeated to herself. Her incredulity shook her head. She crumpled the paper and put her hands on her hips, poised, planning her next move. She sprung up and grabbed the phone.

"O'Hara agency," the voice crackled on the other end of the line.

"Yes. I'd like you to arrange some travel for me please. I need a round trip ticket to Newcastle, then ground transport to and from Kawanga." She scribbled the information on the empty envelope.

"If I'm still leaving tonight, then I've got to pack, and quick," she ordered herself.

A flurry of activity followed: hands in and out of drawers, feet bounding up and down stairs, zippers zipping and buttons buttoning. The door slammed leaving the chain swinging, unemployed. The smell of a badly tuned Holden and the slipping of tires on gravel sent Harriet on her way.

Soon, she was looking out of the plane window, pensively

considering what lay in front of her and remembering her past with Donald Brant. He mind went back to the time he was going through a "kata" by the bed while she busied herself folding clothes. She remembered picking up and sniffing one of his shirts, only to throw it down and then spin around and face him in exasperation at evidence at yet another of his sexual dalliances.

She shouted, "Donald, not again...not again! Why are you doing this to us?"

Weakly he'd responded, "Harri, what? Not 'what' again?"

She'd quickly countered with, "This is *not* my perfume!"

He'd sighed in defeat that time. "I'm sorry; it's not like I plan these things. I was teaching the ladies' class and...well...."

She'd cut him off. "Why explain? Another lady police officer needed private lessons, right? How many times does this have to happen?"

He'd turned her around to face him, embraced her and spoke over her shoulder. "Oh, Harri, I am sorry...really I am. Let's take a few weeks off. We'll go away...to Auckland, to anywhere. I'll forget martial arts and...."

"What, I'll forget about your lack of self-control?"

He shrugged, impishly. "I'm an athlete...I'm just a physically active guy. I was a champion for God' sake, remember?" He flexed his arms as he squeezed her to him.

"I remember," she purred as they kissed.

Misty-eyed at the memory, she came out of her reverie, pouted and folded her arms in a feeble attempt at "righteous indignation." She resumed her gaze out the window.

CHAPTER THIRTEEN

The sunlight slapped him in the face. It was different than England. This was white, not yellow. Bonnington had been amused to hear the pilot announce, minutes before landing, "Well, folks, we're only eight miles from paradise." And then a few minutes later, "Ladies and gentlemen, we're only ten minutes from heaven. If you see a group of people smiling uncontrollably as you disembark, it'll be your flight crew. Enjoy your stay in Sydney."

"From a penal colony to this?" he asked himself as he stood on the hot pavement outside the international terminal. He thought about the two-year waiting list holding many British citizens at bay.

"Maybe this is heaven," he laughed to himself.

* * * * * * *

Harriet stood outside of the taxi, leaned toward the window and asked the driver, "And you think this is the most likely one?"

"It's the only one, Ma'am," he responded with a twinkle in his eye. "Not exactly the best place for a lady to frequent, if you get me drift," he added, winking.

"Thank you, thank you very much, indeed," she said, filling his fist with money. "I'll call in the morning for my ride back."

"Sure thing."

He left her and her bag standing in front of the Dew Drop Inn. She looked pathetic, like a little lost girl from a children's book, alone, there in the moonlight. She turned and looked up at the shabby building's second floor.

* * * * * * *

Bonnington held his empty glass up to his eyes. He peered through its filmy residue, gathering his thoughts. "Can't beat their pubs," he admitted to himself. He couldn't walk one city block without finding a fresh watering hole.

"Another, sir?" the bartender interrupted. He looked more like a barber, or college professor. His slicked hair parted in the middle; he sported a clipped moustache and looked a good deal younger than his years. His face was ruddy, his eyes bright blue; they twinkled, inviting conversation.

"Same thing again," responded the ex-cop.

"Staying awhile?" asked the thin, red-faced man.

"Depends," said Bonnington. "Looking for someone. Kind of a 'macho' type, free-lancer. Supposed to be some kind of martial arts champ. *Former* champ, I think it is, former competitor."

"Brant, Donnie Brant, he must be. Fourth-dan Tae Kwon Do, he is. Yeah, he quit competing, years ago; but he's still a legend, retired undefeated, he did. Donnie Brant, he could move his feet, he could."

"Is he still around, in Sydney?" asked Bonnington, trying on nonchalance.

"S'pose so, s'pose so. Did some commercials, wrote a book, you know, self-defense, for women and kids 'n stuff. He was lucky, not like some of them. Reckon he quit with a pile of money; you know, counting everything, titles, books and all. Donnie Brant, yeah, he's still kind of a local hero. Yeah, s'pose he still lives around these parts; don't hear much about him anymore...yeah, Donnie Brant...yeah...." His voice trailed off, as he wiped shot glasses absentmindedly.

"Thanks, Mate," Bonnington said, tipping his hat.

"No worries," the bartender quipped.

He leaned over and whispered to the burly bridge worker as Bonnington left the bar, "Pommie twit."

They both exploded into laughter.

CHAPTER FOURTEEN

"I'll bet he's getting a shower," she wagered herself, biting her bottom lip. Harriet marched right up to the counter, energized by aggravation. "Do you have a Donald Brant here?" she asked, poker-faced.

"No. 12, upstairs," the red-faced manager replied, jerking his thumb upward.

She touched the doorknob, gingerly; the door was unlocked. It swung open with only the slightest hint of a creak. Once inside, she pushed it closed with her high heel. Water was pouring over a 6' 3" ex-karate tournament competitor in a run-down shower next to the dingy bedroom. She kicked her shoes off and plopped down in the center of the bed, interlaced her fingers behind her brown hair; the spread was cool against her knuckles.

The bathroom door swung open and Brant barged into the bedroom, clad in a gray towel, with a hole in it over the left knee.

"Harriet!" he exclaimed, smoothing his wet, blond hair back. "What are you doing here? How on earth did you find me?" He yanked the chair over and straddled it, in front of the bed.

"Don't pretend to be surprised, Donald. I got your bloody 'package.' What's this supposed to be, some sort of a joke? You call me, tell me an important letter's coming; I get to the post office and the blooming emergency is a blank piece of paper with 'Kawanga' typed on it. It's capers like these that remind me why I divorced you!"

He leaned forward, resting his elbows on the chair back. "Look, there's a lot more to this, a whole helluva lot more. I wrote that note in case...in case I didn't make it; I nearly didn't. This afternoon I was left for dead by some 'rumdumbs' out in the desert. If it hadn't been for one's 'conscience,' if you can believe that, I'd still be there, dying: dying in the bloody desert."

Harriet sat up and swung her legs around the side of the bed, looking at the wall.

"What do you mean, 'more'?" she asked the wall.

"You've no idea, really, no idea, Babe. Let me get dressed; we'll go downstairs and have a meal."

"I swear, Donald Brant; I swear. The things you get me involved in," she said, turning toward him. We can eat a little later. But first...." She slid over to the edge of the bed.

"Harriet; after the day I've had," he protested.

She put her arms around his neck, pulling him to her, kissed him so hard he felt her teeth. He left the towel on the chair.

CHAPTER FIFTEEN

Tom broke out in goose bumps as he lowered himself into the near-scalding bathtub water. He gasped as the water shocked his bruised ribs. At least he was home, alive. He had time to think, to plan, to figure his way out of the past few months, to get back to normal.

He leaned back in the tub; sweat poured from his forehead. He sighed the relief of one who has cheated death. A sigh Camille had been denied.

"He's going to kill all of us," he thought to himself, rubbing a wet finger over his bottom lip. "He tried once; he'll do it again. Harley's not going to leave anyone alive. He's determined to tie up all the loose ends.

"Damn him!" he grunted. "Brant's gone; and Camille; I'll bet he's gotten to Camille. He's going to kill me, Toby, Jim... Harriet. My God, he's going to kill Harriet," he shuddered.

"I didn't do anything wrong; not really," he assured himself. He had been, "down under" for a few weeks, on business. He hadn't the slightest notion of a "whirlwind" courtship: especially not with a karate champion's ex!

But it had happened, hadn't it? With everything against it, it had happened anyway. And he had lost control of his life... and his convictions. He remembered the Sunday School story of David and Bathsheba...how the king hadn't really killed the woman's husband—not directly—just put him in the front line of the battle, so Israel's enemies could do it for him.

"God!" he thought. "Murder *and* adultery!" he said, lashing himself with fresh guilt.

He couldn't imagine broaching the subject with Anne. He wouldn't even let her know he was back in the country for another couple of days.

His mind traveled back to a downtown library in Sydney, Australia. He had approached the pert, vivacious young woman while she was busy with paperwork.

"Excuse me, but where would I find the latest information on the international applications of computer networking?" he'd asked her with his best bland expression.

"You're American," she'd replied. "Down here on business or pleasure?"

"So far, just business; but I'm hoping that will change."

She smiled and responded, "I think you'll find everything you're looking for over in aisle seven."

With an impish smile, he countered with, "Are you sure there's nothing for me here?"

"That depends," she retorted.

"On what?"

"On whether you're interested in what Sydney's *really* like."

"Are you volunteering as my tour guide?"

Quickly, she responded with, "Are you going to pay for dinner? Are you off anytime soon?"

With that, she gathered her purse, stepped around the desk and joined him. They left the lobby together and began making small talk. It turned out she'd been tossed out of her husband's heart by "flying sidekicks" and "heavy bag workouts." Tom had never been unfaithful to Anne; Harriet had never cheated on Donald, although he had not returned the favor. It was a "chemical attraction." Her years of neglect and his years of boredom had met and married in a weekend of unbridled passion. But for all that, he could sense Brant, in her eyes and in her arms. She still loved him, their divorce notwithstanding. If only he were gone—out of the picture—leaving only him and Harriet. And so he had let a retired seaman—one he had met at a pub—convince him to drive an unconscious former athlete to a rendezvous with the cruel Australian elements.

He lay there in the tub, his face covered with perspiration as he remembered more of their relationship. They had had dinner at a restaurant high atop the Centre Point Mall, the city lights gleaming outside their window. He'd asked her, "So, what was it like being married to a famous athlete?"

"Let's put it this way: *we* didn't seem to have enough privacy, but Donald...and other women...lots of them...did."

"I'm sorry," he replied, "I didn't mean to bring up an uncomfortable memory. It's just that, well, I hardly know you and I have this urge to spill my guts and tell you all my 'secrets'."

Her eyes moistened as she asked, "Do you have secrets?"

"Not really; just a loveless marriage. Actually, this trip came at a good time. We—Anne and I—are very close to a divorce. Thought the space might help us think things through."

Her brows furrowed. "And what have you come up with?"

"Anne and I deserve to be happy: both of us. I just don't think it means being together anymore."

"Divorce doesn't need to be angry or messy. You can even remain friends...really...Donald and I get along better since we split up. I know we're both happier."

He leaned back, sighed, looking around the restaurant with a vacant expression. "I don't know. I guess I'm old-fashioned or too straight-laced or something, but I have trouble getting my mind around the concept of divorce."

With that she laughed. "You sound like a fair-dinkum 'Moral Majority' American, for God's sake! I'll bet you went to Sunday School."

He smiled at that one. "I did. I even won perfect attendance pins. But seriously, I've always figured, you make your bed and you lie down in it."

"Tom, I like you; I really do. Would you like to stop by my place on the way home? Just for a quick drink? I really don't want to be alone just now."

He pursed his lips and sighed, "This is all happening kind of quickly."

He and Harriet had entered the dark house together. She locked the door and turned on one small lamp. He embraced and kissed her before she even removed her coat. She pulled off his sport coat and moved to the couch. He turned off the light without breaking their kiss.

But then he remembered the controlled countenance Harriet had sported the last time he had seen her. He winced to recall the shame, the humiliation he'd felt as she'd dictated his "dear John" letter to his face. How it was conveniently "over"; he'd left her and the country that very day.

He wiggled his toes in the water now, changing the scene in his mind.

"What if Brant had given it to Camille?" he mused. "What if the document—the damned piece of paper—that was so important to Harley, important enough to kill for, what if Brant had somehow gotten it to her, before Harley had gotten to him? "What then?"

The question remained unanswered.

He pulled the drain plug.

Tom got out of the tub now, slipped on a bathrobe and exited the bathroom. He entered the bedroom and sat on the edge of the bed where his suitcase lay open, papers strewn over the spread. He picked up various photos of him and Harriet: at Manly Pier, outside the Sydney Opera House, and near other historic landmarks. Frustrated and guilty, he threw them down.

"Damn you, Harley! Adultery and murder!"

He picked up an envelope full of Australian currency. His mind traveled back in time to his visit to The Black Steer, a pub in the heart of Blacktown, a suburb of Sydney. He sat at the bar, nursing a beer, motioning to the counterman to bring him another.

* * * * * * *

"What the hell, better to drink alone than to just *be* alone, right?" The barkeep nodded. Harley was at the other end of the bar, sizing him up as a possible addition to his other company of "employees."

"Whatch drinkin', Yank?" Harley growled.

"Beer," Tom replied.

"So what's the lonely caper about? Drinkin' to forget somethin'?"

"Some*one*. I'm drinking to forget someone. I just got the brush off, direct and personal."

Harley slid off the stool and sat next to him. They looked at each other in the mirror. "Aw, women, Mate. Ain't nothin' on this ol' earth can figure 'em, right?"

Tom mumbled, "Don't wanna figure 'em; wanna forget, period."

Harley sniffed, "I heard that." He turned and offered his rough hand and they shook. "Name's Harley."

"Tom...and thanks for the beer," he replied, tipping his bottle at him.

"No worries. So what's the deal? Who's the Babe?"

Tom raised his glass in another mock toast. "Harriet... Harriet...ex-Brant, ex-Karate champion's ex-wife who isn't really 'ex,' 'cause he's still in her eyes when she's kissing me...."

Just then, a tough Aussie seated near Tom got up and readied himself to smash him with a strong right hand.

"Why you bloomin' Siss; cryin' in your beer over some 'Sheila.' Why, I reckon I'll give you somethin' to cry about!"

At that, Harley sprang up, caught the tough's right fist in his left hand, spun it around and down and "clothes-lined" him off of his barstool.

A startled Tom shouted, "Holy hell; what's his problem?!"

Harley sat back down, took a long pull on his beer and said, "Don't have one now, does he? Reckon he'll just sleep it off, eh?"

Mouth agape Tom mumbled, "I...ah...owe you one."

Harley responded quickly. "Maybe you can do me a favor someday. You stayin' here long?"

"Just a few more days."

Harley raised his beer in a toast. "And a few more beers."

The two men touched bottles as the man lay unconscious at their feet.

* * * * * *

Bringing his mind back to the present, Tom continued to hold the envelope, weighing it in his hand, a look of disgust on his face as he muttered to himself, "Some favor. Harley, you bastard, you; I swear I'll find a way out of this."

The currency spilled out of the envelope onto the bedspread.

CHAPTER SIXTEEN

To be sure, Harley loved her, in a way: a physical, obsessive, erotic way. But an emotion that strong, that close to the edge, could turn to hate, and rage and murder, with one too many drinks.

Harley sat there, on the edge of the dock, sleeves rolled up, elbows resting on his knees. He was a caricature: the old man and the sea. He rubbed his scraggly chin, reached up and threw his smelly hat into the water. His seventy plus years had not once allowed him to get below a surface existence. Emotionally, he was afraid of the water. People, places, circumstances, were all to perish with the using. He lived one step above nature, using intuition instead of instinct. His entire relationship with Camille—such as it was—had been discarded. He had pitched it into a sea of forgetfulness to float to some distant shore, like his hat.

Use, abuse, lose: Harley's modus operandi.

He uncorked the bottle, tilted his head back, and drank one long drink.

* * * * * * *

They drove to the office together now. But it was different. An invisible partition separated C.J. from Rita, a wall made of jealousy: impenetrable, immovable. She sensed it, but wouldn't say it. He felt it, but wouldn't fight it. An emotional wedge pierced the arm rest, dividing and conquering. His mind was an

X-rated cinema featuring non-stop films of Rita and her "lord." His insides churned with every frame.

"C.J., what did I do; what did I say, wrong?"

"Nothing."

"What do you mean?"

"Nothing; don't be ridiculous," he replied, his eyes glued to the traffic in front of him.

Rita sighed and looked out the window, pouting, remonstrating with herself, inwardly.

"Something's wrong; I know something's wrong."

"Look, Rita; I just need some time to think; this whole thing is happening so quickly, I just need to get my bearings, that's all. Just give me a little space, a little time. O.K?"

She smiled, hopeful. "O.K., Hon; O.K."

CHAPTER SEVENTEEN

The shower and what followed made him feel almost, "born again." He was that refreshed. Harriet followed Brant down the wooden stairs into the dinky restaurant. A handful of coarse looking middle-aged "blue-collar" workers sat at the bar, sipping bronze-colored relief from frosty mugs. One elderly couple sat at a table near a window, having a late-night "cuppa."

Brant eyed the room and guided Harriet to a corner table. The bartender appeared, wrapped in a soiled apron.

"So what's it for yous two?" asked the pudgy, bald-headed Aussie.

"Two mixed grills, Mate. Lots of chips and gravy."

"Back in a few." He sauntered back towards the kitchen, leaving Brant and Harriet to discuss the bizarre happenings of the last few days. Donald smiled matter-of-factly at his ex-wife, looking over her shoulder at the hulk of a man at the bar, the one whose eyes advertised a steely hatred of the former tournament competitor.

Exasperated, Harriet said, "Donnie, what's wrong? I know that look; don't tell me someone's giving you that 'damned look.' I swear if you wind up fighting...."

"No worries, Pet. Now, where were we?" he smiled impishly.

"What's been going on? You were going to tell me about you being in the desert, and what's the story on this town, the note; what's going on?"

She leaned forward, trying to get every nuance of meaning.

The man at the bar snickered, looked at the ceiling, draining his mug.

Brant inhaled deeply, through his nose, exhaled slowly, through barely parted lips. He rolled his fingers up into a tightly clenched fist, folded his thumb over his first two fingers.

"Oh, no," she said, folding her arms in front of her on the table, laying her head onto her forearms.

The big man slowly spun off the stool, eased himself up to his full large frame and pulled his jeans up, over the small paunch creeping over his belt. He lumbered over to the table, put his hands on his hips and challenged Brant.

"Ya know, I never thought you was much at all. That oriental stuff...to me it's sissy crap. ' The way I get it, only sheilas fights with their feet. Know what I mean, Sport?" He folded his arms in front of him, defiant.

Harriet looked up. "You're making the biggest mistake you've made all week."

"'Sat so, Lady? That what you think, Guv?"

Brant inhaled, exhaled again, slowly, inaudibly. He straightened himself; both men squared off, striking traditional boxing poses.

"I don't fancy fighting for free, Mate. But, hell, can't have you calling me a 'Sheila' in fronta me girl, can I"? He winked out of the corner of his right eye at Harriet.

Before his challenger had fully cocked his fist back, Brant's right leg spun forward, the inside of his shoe striking his opponent's left temple. Before the giant had fallen, Donnie spun completely around, whipping his left boot-heel into the man's left jaw. The giant collapsed like a felled tree with a thud, unconscious, his mouth full of blood and loose teeth.

"Still got it, eh Pet?" Brant smiled. "Bartender...we'll take the food up to our room. This chap's nearly put me off me meal."

The pudgy man leaned over the bar, open-mouthed.

"Right-e-o, Mr. Brant. Have it right upstairs in a jiff." He wiped his bald head with a dish towel. The elderly couple left; the others at the bar looked straight ahead, as though the glass rack were a television set.

Brant looked out of the window into the black night, his right boot braced on the sill. "Sometimes I still miss it, Harri. Fighting professionally, I mean; can't beat it, the competition."

"Forget the fighting, Donnie. What's going on"?

He turned around, smiled and plopped into the faded chair. The bartender arrived, slid the tray onto the table and exited, without turning around.

"So...where are we?" he asked themselves, pursing his lips.

"Yes, where are we?" Harriet demanded.

"Geez, it's a long story, Pet. Crazy, really; bloody nuts." He filled his mouth with sausage and continued talking, munching.

He put his fork down, looking straight into her green eyes. "It's like this. I was in this pub, outside of Blacktown. I meet this old rummy, you know, sailor-type, retired. Anyway, he's talkin' to some of the chaps 'bout his old 'war stories,' sea legends 'n such. I'm within earshot, having a brew, and, hell, he's real friendly...recognized me...says, 'Brant, here's one 'might interest you."

Harriet mixed the fried potatoes with thick gravy, spellbound at her former husband's story.

"Anyway," he continued, with a mouthful of egg and vegetables; "Seems this old goat—Harley's his name—this codger's got some legend 'bout a legal document related to the settling of Australia. He'd had too much to drink, really started spilling his guts...about how if the Aborigines only knew...."

"Knew what?"

"That's what I couldn't get out of the old sot at first. Hell, you know me and the Aboriginals; I've trained 'em. They make good fighters if they're trained right. Anyway, I followed him back to his room, tried to draw him out. He tells me there's a document—somewhere in England—in some lord or other's house vault. Anyway, he laughs and says this document is actually a valid legal paper deeding some Australian land to the Aborigines."

Harriet gasped and gaped, "What?!

"Yeah, giving some Aussie land to the Aboriginals. Don't

that beat it all?" he asked, shaking his head.

"Now, get this. I says to him, if this is for real...if such a document really exists...do you have any idea of the general area involved, the general area?"

"Then he wheezed and squinted and pierced me with his eyes, like he was looking way down into me socks. He licked some whiskey from his lips and says, "No, I can't give you a general idea, boy, I can give you an exact idea, a specific location. It's bloody Sydney!"

Brant dropped his silverware; Harriet gulped.

They looked at each other in astonishment and blurted out in unison..., "Sydney!"

CHAPTER EIGHTEEN

If Australia was the "land down under," Perth was another planet. Thousands of miles separated Harley from Jim and Toby. At last they could relax. Actually, the two brothers had enjoyed their trans-continental flight, luxuriating in the efficient air conditioning. The beers had done a lot toward removing the edge from their tension: Harley's threats were fading. They stood outside the terminal, preparing for the taxi cab ride to their destination.

"Epley hotel," Jim barked as he and Toby tossed their bags into the cab and followed them in.

"Right, Mates," the red-faced driver replied, looking in the rear view mirror.

"Got these flamin' lights figured, Mates. Just hit this intersection right and do bloody sixty all the way; no worries," he laughed.

The speedometer was magnetized to sixty kilometers per hour. The boys watched the scenery speed by, looked at each other and smiled.

"God, it'll be good to be back in Perth. At least we can get back to normal; one thing's for sure; we know the bloody job. We can just pick up where we left off, Mate. Once a deck hand, always a deck hand."

Jim ran his fingers through his curly, blond hair and looked back out the window.

Toby let his head fall back against the stained seat cushion.

"Guess Brant's a memory by now; Tom got rid of him, eh?"

"Mmm," Jim responded. "Forget Brant; forget the whole damned thing. It just didn't work out."

"Yeah. Hell, it was a long shot anyway, right?"

"Too right," said Jim with a nod.

Neither of the boys ever saw the truck that rammed their cab, head on. There was a blast of body odor as the heavy cabbie jerked the wheel, then a bang followed by a shrill screech of metal, the truck's attempt to gobble the cab like one ancient dinosaur devouring another.

The old truckie looked into his rear view mirror as he continued racing down the barren stretch of road. His sunburned forehead creased as he muttered, "Greetings from Harley, Mates. He's got friends everywhere, Sports; got friends everywhere."

* * * * * * *

Bonnington was getting nowhere, fast.

He had exhausted just about all of the leads he had been able to muster. The town's people weren't talking. After all, for them he was desecrating a relic, one of Blacktown's only claims to fame. And he was a "Pommie," an Englishman, a rude reminder of the country's unsophisticated beginnings. "Prisoner of Mother England," he quipped. "Bloody Aussies," he answered himself.

He sat in the shiny, blue Commodore, wishing he could make it disappear and then reappear in England, to take the place of the old Leyland he'd settled for.

"Bloody Aussies," he said to himself again, owning his jealousy.

His fingers played an imaginary piano piece on the stationary steering wheel while his mind replayed his first conversation with Lord Conley. The pompous fat man was understandably humiliated to discover that his wife was seeing another man, and an Australian at that!

* * * * * * *

Bonnington stood in front of Conley's desk, apprehensive.

The old man motioned with his meaty hand, "Please, sit down. Tell me all of it."

The detective reluctantly took a seat opposite his host. He sat there squirming and fidgeting.

Conley reiterated. "And I mean all of it."

"I've...ah...located Mrs. Conley, Sir."

"Well, out with it, Man. Come, come now. I'm paying you to discover the truth, the whole lot...regardless of any embarrassment you feel it may cause me."

"As you wish, Sir. It seems Mrs. Conley is keeping company with...an Australian. A former martial arts champion, named Donald Brant. He's only been here in England a short time."

He recalled the look of disdain on Conley's face as he related Camille's sexual shenanigans.

The old man looked away, sighed, talking to Bonnington while gazing out the window.

"I see. Well, I can't expect her to be completely satisfied with someone my age...even with my financial status."

The detective countered with, "I don't really understand their relationship, Sir. Perhaps it is strictly a physical infatuation."

"No doubt. She's done this before; she'll do it again. I knew that when I brought her home with me from France. The important thing is that you've located her."

Bonnington nodded weakly.

"I'm not sure about this Brant fellow, but I am sure Camille is the key to retrieving the document I've referred to. I'm standing by my offer. Find that article and I shall pay you one hundred fifty thousand pounds."

"I understand, Sir. And I will find the paper...even if it means traveling halfway around the world. That money means an awful lot to me."

Conley smiled. "Oh, I know it does. And that document means an awful lot to me: much more than does Camille."

* * * * * * *

His mind back in the present moment, Bonnington tightened his hands on the steering wheel.

He mused about Rita's "unofficial" relationship with Brant. The detective remembered how he had secretly enjoyed seeing the conceited Conley discover someone—Rita—whose affections he couldn't buy. But it wasn't as simple as a mischievous mistress or a wandering wife. There was the paper, the document, the missing deed that Conley had been willing to part with one hundred fifty thousand pounds in order to have returned. And that money was Bonnington's future; nothing and no one would keep him from it: certainly not an Australian ex-karate competitor.

His mind traveled thousands of miles in a few seconds. He was back in Blacktown. Little children giggled and gurgled in the park to his left. His stomach churned and burned as he sat and stewed. He had to find Brant: find him and pull the answers out of him, if need be. This was not just a job, this was retirement, a happy ending to a sad story he'd told himself all of his life.

He smiled from his car window at the children playing on the swing set.

"Play fair, now" he said to them. "Take turns, why don't you?"

The children paused their playing to look up at him, then at each other, and then began to laugh and continue their games.

He snickered, started the engine, put the car in gear and eased away from the curb and down the main thoroughfare, toward Brant, toward the answers, toward his financial reward, toward his "happy ending."

The children again paused in their playing; they watched as the shiny, blue car rolled down the street.

And they laughed.

CHAPTER NINETEEN

C.J. and Rita tumbled onto the living room floor. One lone lamp lit the room causing shadows to loom like silent spectators. Rita lay on her back, looking up, wary but hopeful. C.J. crouched beside her. He leaned over her and put his hands on her shoulders, gently pinning her to the carpet. He'd always liked that beige turtleneck; he enjoyed the feel of it under his hands.

"C.J., are we finally going to talk?"

He sat up, his arms behind him, leaning on his palms. Rita sat up and stared into his eyes in the semi-darkness.

"Yeah, we're going to talk. I just need to know more about England, about this "lord.""

Rita burst out with a laugh and a sigh. "So that's what this has all been about? England? Lord Conley? C.J., I can't believe it...you're...you're jealous!"

"So what if I am?" he exclaimed. A great crack had been forged in the wall that separated them. He was amazed at the relief he felt. The emotional ice was thawing.

"Honey, I told you; it was over almost as soon as it started. I was working in the consulate and I was introduced to this lord—Conley—at a party. He was a widower and I was, well, lonely, and new to England and so anxious to succeed. C.J.," she blurted out, "it didn't mean anything; don't let him come between us. Don't let a few weeks ruin this...our future."

Her eyes pleaded with him like a little girl pining for the one doll she couldn't live without.

He reached for her, put his hands on her shoulders, drew her head to his chest and covered her with his arms. He looked into the empty fireplace. "I love you, Rita. Love you like I've never loved anyone or anything. I just need to know that I have all of you."

She pulled back and looked into his eyes again.

"You do, C.J.; God, you do."

He reached over and turned out the lamp as they kissed.

* * * * * * *

The kettle whistled while Rita poured the hot chocolate mix into the chipped porcelain cups. The kitchen was cheery; depression was simply impossible there.

"Mmmm, that smells great," he said as he poured in the steaming water. Rita slid the macaroons out of their wrapper and pushed two toward his side of the table. The vapor from the cocoa opened his sinuses as he sipped the sweet drink. They looked at each other, smiling, munching.

"C.J.," she mused, holding a cookie in front of her eyes. "There is something else you should know." She put the macaroon down and looked at him.

"Really, about Conley?"

"Sort of. It's kind of, well complicated," she said as she turned her own head in disbelief.

"Remember I told you Conley was a widower? Well, that wasn't exactly true. His first wife had died, but he had remarried; I didn't find out till I had stopped seeing him. Anyway, there was this other man...I didn't see him romantically," she reassured him, trying to circumvent yet a new pain for him.

"He was an Australian. He turned out to be one of their martial arts champions. He was looking for information about which members of the English government might be responsible for liaison work with Australia. He was interested in information about land rights and the settling of the country. I told him I didn't have much information for him since I was involved with the American consulate but that coincidentally, I had just met a Lord Conley at a party, and that he had something to do with Anglo-Australian relations."

"So what?" asked C.J., hunting for a connection in the story to his relationship with Rita.

"Well, he came back, once or twice, almost like he was giving me an update, you know, on his progress. Like he felt he owed me some follow up. Maybe he liked me," she smiled, taunting C.J.

He clicked his tongue.

She slapped his forearm and laughed. "You...jealous; I still can't believe it."

CHAPTER TWENTY

Bonnington slipped into Harriet's apartment with the ease of a cat burglar. "Looks like a bomb went off," he muttered to himself. He quickly scanned the living room, eyed the phone stand and picked up the folded piece of typing paper.

"Kawanga? Sounds like a bloomin' animal. Kawanga? Must be an outback town. What the hell's in Kawanga? And who did this?" he asked himself as he surveyed the damage.

After he made his way back outside, he opened up the map on the front seat of his car and illuminated the Sydney area with his flashlight. His big finger made several circles before lighting on a small black dot, almost directly west of Sydney. He sat there, tapping the spot on the page.

"Kawanga!"

* * * * * * *

There was nothing more to do but wait. But it was the waiting that unnerved him, undermined him, destroyed his confidence with every passing day. He was alone in a crowded country. Every day was colored by a thick gray cloud of fear and apprehension. His affair with Rita had all but faded from memory. But the deed, the very thought of it sent an electric shock of stinging fear and guilt through his overweight frame. His palms perspired; his stomach tingled.

Lord Conley paced the grounds mindlessly. He again tried to solace himself by recounting Bonnington's experience and the motivation of the money. He took deep breaths of the English air. Presently, Anderson ambled over to him, his affect as solicitous as always.

"Sleep any better last evening, Sir?"

Startled from his reverie, Conley responded. "Not really, Anderson. I'm not certain I'll sleep very comfortably until this entire matter is settled, one way or the other."

"Is it Miss Rita?" the servant inquired, his eyebrows arched in anticipation of a solid response of some kind. The huge man sighed. "If only it were Miss Rita. No, it's the damned piece of paper. Can you imagine that, Anderson? A single piece of paper is rendering me a prisoner in this palace, a convict, unconfined?"

"I'm afraid I don't understand, Sir."

Conley snickered, "No, you don't, Anderson; no one would."

"But Detective Sergeant Bonnington, Sir, surely he won't disappoint you."

The British lord looked at Anderson, then away at his grounds. After several deep breaths he smiled. "No, he won't. He's too well trained and he's got too much at stake."

"A retirement pension or some such, wasn't it?"

"Yes. Something I should think you would be concerned about."

Anderson smiled impishly. "Oh, I don't know, Sir. You've been awfully good to me, awfully good."

"And you to me, Anderson."

The two men faced each other, unequal in stature but remarkably equal in nature, a horse grazing in the background. The dutiful servant slowly made his way back to the house.

Again, Conley's fears began to dissipate. Bonnington would not fail. The sunlight splashed over him as he walked out from under a great oak tree. He inhaled again. He exhaled and leaned his weight against the tree.

He daydreamed of a distant island-continent.

CHAPTER TWENTY-ONE

Harriet and Brant were finishing their coffee while he went about finishing his story. It was past midnight.

"Well, where is the deed?" Harriet asked.

"You find Conley and get involved with his wife—if I had a dollar for every time you've been unfaithful—what did she do with the deed?"

"Harri, like I told you, first of all, there was nothing between us—Camille and me—it was just a brief, physical thing. What can I say, she was that kind of girl; don't know how in the world she ever tied up with Conley, maybe the old duffer was going senile.

"She was a feisty little tart. Didn't take her long at all to find her way into his personal affairs. Well, even a girl with her limited background could understand the main gist of the paper; it actually deeded the area of Sydney to the Aborigines. You can imagine the wheels that started turning in her head then. If one thing makes Camille tick, it's 'jack': money's all she's really interested in."

"How did you get it?" Harriet asked, sipping the cappuccino.

"Well I didn't at first," he interrupted.

"She had it in her mind to blackmail Conley; she knew the absolutely catastrophic consequences that would develop if word of that piece of paper ever got anywhere near the wrong people."

"So how did you get her to part with it, Donnie?" Harriet's eyes widened, waiting for his reply, trying to make some sense out of his story.

Brant took a long drink of coffee, smacked his lips and stretched; he smoothed his hair back and closed his eyes, leaning back in his chair. He began to describe the images that he saw in his mind's eye, scenes that portrayed the events of the past week.

* * * * * * *

Camille and Brant were sitting at a table working on their dinners. He looked up from his plate, set his silverware down and said, "Okay, let's see it." She eyed him across the table, cautiously. Reluctantly, slowly, she slid the deed over to him. His blue eyes carefully scanned it for a few moments.

"Un-bloody-believable! It's 'fair-dinkum' all right. Can you believe it?"

Her eyes widened and the sun came up in with her smile.

"Yes, I believe it, of course I believe it. Donnie, let's make some money!"

He sighed and slapped the document with his palm. "I've already told you, that's not possible."

Perplexed, she responded, "Why? Why, 'that's not possible'?"

He leaned forward. "Camille, think. You're an illegal French alien. The only reason you're in England is because of Conley. It's too dangerous."

Exasperated, she asked, "Why? What's the danger?"

He pursed his lips, replied, "The 'danger' is I've been followed. Face it: Conley's not going to suspect anyone but you of the theft. Whoever is tailing us is after you; I'm just a side issue in this caper. By the way, how on earth did you do it anyway?"

The French vixen smiled coyly as she described her and Conley's drunken night of carousing and debauchery. "I got him drunk and 'sexed him up;' It was not difficult, really."

"And?"

"We danced, the two of us, three sheets to the wind, until he fell on the bed, unconscious, his dressing gown in disarray."

Brant sat silently, waiting for the missing details.

"It was then that I noticed a small mark on his leg. He had the combination to the safe tattooed on the inside of his thigh; his memory was already failing him in many ways."

Donnie shook his head in disgust.

"Later I tiptoed downstairs, across the hall to his study. I carefully slid the painting away and there was the safe, just waiting for me. I quickly rustled through papers, bonds and jewelry, until I found a yellowed parchment with an official-looking seal on it."

Brant offered, "Well, you can forget about blackmail. It's too risky; not possible. You don't fancy spending the rest of your life in a "Pommie" prison, do you?"

Camille sighed, played with her food, disgusted and disappointed in Brant's apparent cowardice.

"Look, Camille. It's no good for you here anymore. Come back with me to Australia. You can start over. I seriously doubt Conley'll ever find you there. I really think it's your only option."

Looking up into his eyes like a petulant little girl she asked, "Why do you want to help me? You love me, don't you. You do love me."

He sighed, "Love's got nothing to do with it. It's just that, well, I owe you. If it weren't for you, I would never have found this." He hefted the deed in his strong right hand.

"This is important; the Aborigines deserve better than what they've gotten. They deserve *this*."

Their wine glasses sat, untouched, in the center of the table, the document speaking volumes with its silent presence.

* * * * * *

And so the two of them, Brant and Camille, along with the deed, left Conley and Bonnington behind when they boarded a plane bound for Sydney at London's Heathrow airport. Two glasses sat on the tray-table in front of them.

Brant spoke quietly, without taking his eyes off of the paper. "There's one more thing, there's a fellow in Sydney, an old man, the one who put me on to this whole wild goose chase; he's a real nasty fellow. Harley's his name. The way I get it, he's interested in nothing but money: money and power. He's a rough one, a real honest-to-god rough one. Keep away from him, especially until I've cleared all this up with the authorities."

Camille looked over at him, flashed her eyes and smiled. She put her palm over his right hand, gently raking her nails over his skin.

"Too bad this plane's so crowded, Donnie. You take such good care of me," she purred. "I'm so grateful...I'd like to show you."

Brant pulled his arm away. "Look, Camille," he said, still not looking up from the paper. "This is strictly business; what's happened between us is over, finished."

She folded her arms in front of her and pouted, "Hmmph."

* * * * * * *

They felt like their legs would never move normally again, even with the various touchdowns en-route from England. There was no easy way to make the trip. But they were there. The two of them grunted and sighed as they plopped into the back seat of the taxi, their eyes drooping with fatigue. The driver spoke with them in the rear view mirror.

"Where to?"

Brant responded mechanically, "3122 Quigley, first floor."

The cabbie smiled and responded, "No hassles; be there in a jiff." With that the vehicle pulled away from the airport terminal and headed off to their destination.

There was nothing remotely similar to conversation between them on the way to Brant's apartment. The door opened and an exhausted Brant and Camille entered. He tossed his bags on the floor while she set hers down just inside the door. Furtively, she looked up, asked, "Well, shall we 'go to bed'?"

Incredulous, he replied, "Don't even think about it! You go on; the bed's straight ahead."

"What about you?" she pouted.

He stood there, hands on his hips, "Darlin', I could sleep right here, standing up."

With that, Camille sighed, disappointed, and made her way into the bedroom. Brant looked around at the familiar surroundings, eyed the inviting carpet and spread out, face-down, on the floor. The clock on the lamp table read 12:05 p.m.

Camille woke about six hours later. She could hear Brant snoring in the living room, still face down on the carpet. She cat-walked over to the door, lifted the edge of the carpet and tucked the deed under; the oriental rug flapped back, guarding its contents. She quietly closed the door behind her.

* * * * * * *

"What was it," Camille asked herself? "The Black...Steer... the Black Steer!" she exclaimed, relieved to remember the name of the pub Donnie had said Harley frequented. In a little over an hour, she was getting out of the train, making her way up the cement stairs, minutes from a brightly illuminated sign announcing The Black Steer.

She recognized Harley, immediately. His spirit seemed to call to her. And he did look dangerous, and powerful. She sat at the table next to his. He leaned over and whispered in his raspy voice, "Buy the lady a drink or a sandwich?"

"Both" she smiled, joining his table.

"My name's Harley," he announced with pride, a grin spreading across his face. "These are some friends of mine: Toby, Jim and this fellow's a Yank: name's Tom."

All three men nodded.

"I wonder if I might talk to you...alone" Camille asked.

"Alone...why sure; let's just slide over to that booth."

He led her to the black booth in the corner. He put both forearms on the table and squinted into her eyes.

"Lady have a name?" His voice sounded like he was used to gargling with gravel.

"Camille; sorry, my name is Camille."

"Right, Camille; now, what's this about then?"

Harley motioned to the waiter who disappeared into the kitchen.

Harley continued, "Have some 'tucker' in a minute."

She smiled artificially and continued with her tale.

"I guess it might be crazy but I met this fellow from here, from Australia, named Donald Brant he's a retired...."

"Karate man," Harley blurted out. "Brant, yeah, he's well known 'round here."

Tom's eyes widened at the mention of Brant's name; he leaned over, as far as his chair would allow.

"Well, to make a long story short, he told me this crazy story about a deed...."

The waiter interrupted, placing two sandwiches and two beers in front of them. They shot him an irritated glance and Camille resumed her story. All the while, Tom watched and listened in the background.

"...a document that deeded the area that's now Sydney back to the Aborigines. He said you were the one who told him about it. Well, I've got it, the deed. I'm married to Lord Conley, the Englishman in whose custody the paper was placed."

She licked her lips and lowered her voice. "I've stolen it; stolen it and come out here, with Brant. He says blackmail would be too dangerous; he plans to just give it to the authorities. But I understand that you're not the fearful type. Can you imagine how much money it could be worth to my husband to keep this all quiet?" she asked.

Harley paused, then exploded with laughter.

"He believed it? Ah...ha...ha...bloody Brant believed it! Lady Conley, whatever your name is, I'm sorry but that story's a load of late night pub rubbish I've been spilling for years. I don't know what kind of paper you think you have but I can tell you it won't stand up anywhere, not even in a 'kangaroo court!'"

Camille's face went white. She sat opposite the rude man open-mouthed, her insides stinging with humiliation.

Harley leaned forward, "So...'avin' a good time with you, is he?" he winked.

She sat there in the black leather booth, dumbfounded. Her mind was frozen, her thoughts numb.

Presently, a burly bridge worker at the bar, noticed Camille's reaction and Harley's whispering, slid off his stool and decided to help one whom he considered a "damsel in distress."

"Look here, Guv, no need to be givin' the lady here 'the Mickey', eh?"

Harley looked up, his smile fading. In one quick motion he broke the beer bottle neck with his left hand while he yanked the man forward by grabbing his belt buckle. He menaced the fellow waving the broken bottle under the man's throat.

Harley spat the words out, "Listen, 'Guv,' I'd just as soon slit yer throat and bleed you like the fat sow you are...so back off!"

The man's friend, from close behind him, attempted to even the score.

"See here, now; this Bloke's me Mate."

At that, Harley sprang up, dropped the bottle and drove the web of his left palm into the burly Aussie's throat, while smashing his friend's jaw with his right elbow. The first man sputtered and fell, clutching his throat. Harley then grabbed his friend by the shirt collar and belt and hoisted him up and over the bar. At the sound of the commotion, the waiter scurried out from the kitchen, trying to restore order.

The red-faced man addressed Harley. "See here, now. We'll have no rough stuff in this restaurant. This ain't no dive, you know."

"And this ain't no 'rough stuff'," Harley replied with finality.

Camille was visibly shaken as the room came back to some semblance of order.

Harley just stared, awaiting Camille's reply to his earlier question about her relationship with Brant. He gave no indication of his inner elation, of his exhilaration at the thought of the blackmail fortune he would make, thanks to his French acquaintance's unwitting help. Something had finally, actually fallen into his lap.

"I...ah, I...really can't talk anymore right now; I've had a long flight...," she stammered. "I need some rest."

"Got just the place, me lady. I've got a little house, not far from here; don't use it much anymore. You're welcome to it; I seriously feel awful bad 'bout what's happened...with Brant and all, I mean. It's the least I can do, really," he said, trying to dispel his repressed laughter.

"I really don't know what to say," she responded weakly, still stunned by the impact of his words.

"Just say 'yes,' and you're apples, Pet" he smiled.

She managed a thin, vacant smile. "Yes."

Camille left the pub with Harley's house keys and a heart full of shattered plans and dreams.

Harley returned to his table where Toby, Jim and Tom were busy finishing their meals.

"Got a little proposition for yous boys; interested?" Harley peeped.

They looked at each other, then at Harley before nodding affirmatively. Harley nodded in Tom's direction.

"Might even have something for you to do down the road, Yank. Whatta ya think?"

Tom looked at the boys, then at Harley.

"Depends."

Harley chuckled. "'Depends'? Yeah, depends. Too right. Well then, let's get down to bidness."

* * * * * * *

The boys entered Brant's living room with quiet profession-alism. A land mine couldn't have awakened him. They searched everywhere for the document destined in Harley's mind to make him rich: rich and powerful beyond his imagination. An hour later they left with nothing.

Meanwhile, Camille leaned against the stone wall outside the restaurant watching with empty eyes as the traffic sped by. Later, in Harley's house, when the phone rang and she slipped the receiver from its cradle she recognized the raspy voice on the other end of the line immediately.

"Uh, Miss Camille, the paper, the one you told me about...do you actually have it...with you in Australia?"

"Yes, it's in a safe place, Mr. Harley. But then, what's the difference; it's not worth the paper it's printed on, right?"

"Fair enough," he coughed. "But even so, I'd love to 'ave a look at it; bet I'd get a belly laugh out of it, eh?"

"Bet you would," she retorted, and hung up the receiver. She gazed out the window, new hope entering her heart.

Harley's insincere disinterest vanished, replaced by a calculating resolve. He slammed the receiver down. He motioned to the door with his head and muttered through near closed teeth, "It's got to be at Brant's. Get it...now."

They looked at each other, then at Harley, then slid hurriedly off their bar stools and left.

The boys approached Brant's apartment with anxiety this time, afraid they would find him awake. Neither of them fancied tangling with the tall, two-hundred-pounder: retired or not.

Inside, Brant was on the phone with Willy, a retired competitor, an Aborigine.

"Right-e-o, so tell me, Willy, there is something to this 'long-lost deed' caper?"

"Papa Wamba, he know 'bout that stuff, Donnie."

"Can you take me there, to see Papa?"

"Willy always help Mr. Brant; Mr. Brant, he always help Willy, try make him champ. Remember?"

Brant smiled, "Yeah, I remember, Mate. Listen, I'll be over in a jiff."

He hung up the receiver just as Jim and Toby kicked open the door.

"'S'cuse us, Mr. Brant," sneered Jim, "but we think you have something we, ah, want."

"That right?" Brant answered, cool as ice.

From a standing position, he leaped into the air, and with his right leg cocked, his foot parallel to his extended left leg, delivered a jumping side kick to Jim's chest, driving him out of the room and into the wall outside. Toby stood motionless and began to urinate.

"How 'bout you, Mate; want to 'ave a go?" Brant smiled.

He pushed the younger brother aside and was down the flight of stairs, in his car, and at the first red light before Jim moved. Toby slumped against the apartment wall and slowly peered outside where his brother lay, unconscious.

CHAPTER TWENTY-TWO

The hut where the medicine man lived was dark. Brant and Willy entered the dusty shack with all the proper respect they could muster.

Papa Wamba crouched against the far wall, fumbling with some beads.

Willy began, "This here's the one I told you 'bout, Papa. Loves us, wants to help our people. Mr. Brant, here, he want know 'bout the paper, 'bout the land, 'bout Sydney s'posed to belong to Aborigines."

The withered old shaman dropped his beads and looked up into the faces of the white man and the black man seeking his wisdom.

"Papa tell you one thing anyhow, Pommies give us land, Sydney land, long time ago. Government man, he's daughter real bad sick. Papa's great-great-grandpapa, he do healin' magic; she get well, tell you one thing anyhow."

Brant interjected, "Papa, this government man, he deeded the land, Sydney, to your people as payment, in gratitude for the healing?"

The old man continued, looking down, trance-like.

"Yeah, he did 'em. But British change mind, hide truth, hide deed. Then my people, they do larbarbidee, they 'point bone' at any one, any time, who keep deed from us. Tell you one thing anyhow; Pommies keep deed, they dyin', sure thing."

"But Papa," Brant interjected, "What if the deed could be returned to you, to the Aboriginal authorities. What if the deed and the land could be returned to you?" asked Brant.

"Ha," the old man laughed and shrugged. "Sydney no good now; too much buildings now, too much smoke. Forget land, just need paper. We get paper, dyin' stop, sure thing."

Brant looked up slowly and turned his head to face Willy. They backed out of the room together, from the darkness into the bright sunlight.

* * * * * * *

Harley sat across the table from Camille. He was clean shaved now and his red hair was slicked back. He looked almost attractive, in a rough, unfinished way. He appeared younger than his years. Camille sipped her drink; she tried to keep the attraction she sensed for him out of her consciousness. It certainly wasn't aesthetic appeal; it was in her nerves and muscles. In a bizarre way, she wanted him.

Camille ran her long fingers through her shoulder-length black hair. Her feline features and lithe figure weren't lost on her guest. His glands and pulse reminded him of many others who had preceded this girl, this young girl, a third his age.

"Listen, Miss Camille," he rumbled. "I feel real bad 'bout all this deed business...really do. But I got the feelin' on the phone when we talked that, well, maybe you still think there's something to it. Well, there just ain't. It's nothin' in the world, and, well, I'd be glad to prove it to you. I'm sure you'd feel an awful lot better if you knew, really knew," he squinted, "that it was plain nothin'."

Her throat was dry; her voice cracked as she whispered her reply.

"I was thinking that, well, maybe you were just trying to get me off the track...to do the blackmailing yourself...to keep all the money," she confessed, with almost childlike innocence.

"Camille," he offered. "May I call you 'Camille'?" he asked. She nodded, her heartbeat quickening. "A girl like you, as attractive as you, well, a girl like you don't happen along too often.

The first day I saw you, at the Black Steer, I felt somethin;' think you did, too. Look, I ain't gettin' any younger. I mean to say that if there were somethin' to all this I would have gotten that deed myself years ago. I got all kinda connections and mates in a lot o' places; know what I mean, Pet? Anyways, I'd've gotten it and tied up with a pretty young thing...like you...a long time ago."

Harley stood up and moved behind her chair. Her pulse was racing now, her breath coming in short gasps. She felt the rough fingers on her neck; his skin was sandpaper.

"How 'bout showin' me this 'deed' and I'll give you an honest rundown on it, no strings. What do you say, pretty lady?"

"It's at Brant's place, under an oriental rug. I'll take you there," she replied, as though she were hypnotized.

She stood and turned to face him. He smiled and pulled her to him. As she looked at his face, it seemed to change, to dissolve into a collage of faces, dozens of them, old ones, like her father's.

In her mind's eye she was a little girl now, looking up, frightened at her father's figure in the semi-darkness. She remembered pleading with him, *"Non...Papa...non."*

* * * * * * *

Bonnington waited in the phone box at the back of the pub. Cigarette smoke filled the room, the rumble of a dozen conversations caused him to press the receiver tighter to his ear. Through the "miracle" of electronics, he and Conley were able to converse though separated physically by cultures and thousands of miles.

"I'm getting close, Sir, awfully close. Seems this whole thing's coming down to a place called Kawanga, a little outback town, west of Sydney. It's awfully close, Sir." he assured the burly man on the other end of the static-laden line.

"Yes, should have it finished up in a matter of hours. Yes, I know, I do need the rest of the money. Right...I'll call before I fly back...give you all the details."

He hung up the receiver and looked at the bar. It mesmerized him. It beckoned to him. For more years than he could remember, it had been more faithful to him than any woman could have been.

He needed a drink.

* * * * * * *

C. J. sat, relaxed, in his leather office chair. He picked up the phone, dialed, paused. At the sound of the answering machine's beep he left the brief message.

"This message is for Rita McCallum."

He smiled, shifting a bit in his chair, looking out the window at the sun-drenched city below.

"Hey, Babe; we are finally an item. 'Uncle Sam' is quite the matchmaker. I'm glad I took this job; glad you did too. I guess this is another one in the books for 'workplace romance.' See you tonight...and hope you get this message. Love you...only."

CHAPTER TWENTY-THREE

A pensive pair, Brant and Willy made their way back to the car. A group of tough, young Aussies were waiting, some sitting on the hood, others leaning against the doors. The leader stood in front, daring and defiant.

Brant smiled, "G'day."

"G'day yourself, Whacha doin' with 'im?" he sneered, motioning to the young Aboriginal at Brant's side. "Now what's that to you, Sport?"

The tough turned with a knowing look to his comrades.

"It's like this: we got our own plans for the likes of 'im." He cast a hateful glance at Willy. "Ain't that right, Mate?"

Willy looked down, humiliated, turned to Brant, unsure of how to proceed.

"Willy," Brant said, "You mean to tell me these 'girls' are the ones who've been shakin' down your people? These blokes are the chumps who've been rippin' your nation off?"

Willy remained silent while all the boys gathered together around him and Brant.

"Willy," Brant continued, "I don't think you'll be needin' that heavy bag workout today. Who knows, we may even work up a sweat!"

At this remark the gang leader charged forward, "Why you...."

The unplanned confrontation didn't last long enough to merit even a single column at the rear of a newspaper's back pages. The defeated attackers lay sprawled out in the sand, hanging over porch railings and on the car's bonnet. The semi-conscious leader lay at Brant's feet in the sand. He knelt down and grabbed the young tough's shirt collar.

"How's it feel? How's it feel to be the prey? How's it feel to be outclassed and outdone?"

The man's eyes lolled around.

"Every time you look at these bruises or feel the pain from this trouncing, you remember: these people deserve better."

Willy looked on, embarrassed but appreciative. Brant resumed his standing posture and faced Willy.

"Like old times, eh Donnie?"

Brant looked down at the leader. "Some things never change."

Willy smiled. "But tomorrow's another day, eh?"

Brant nodded. "Yeah. Hopefully a new day."

He put his arm around Willy's shoulder as they made their way to the car.

* * * * * * *

The office was different now, as though work and play had merged together. Their relationship colored every aspect of their experience of life. Their whole world was a stage and they were playing lovers, continuously.

He pushed the copy room door open just as a petite blond over the machine yelled, "Damn this thing! I can never get this thing to make two clean copies in a row!"

She slammed the lid and looked up at C.J., embarrassed.

"Something wrong?" he asked the slightly bottom-heavy girl. "Anything I might be able to help you with?"

He ran his finger between his neck and collar; his pulse seemed quicker. She seemed aware of his attention and at the same time, intrigued by it.

She spoke softly, "This could be trouble."

Catching her double-meaning, he paused slightly before replying. "I know."

CHAPTER TWENTY-FOUR

Hours seemed like days; Tom was glued to the hotel room couch. His mind was foggy, fuzzy with fear and guilt. He couldn't break free of what he'd done to Brant. Now he was beginning to regret the affair with Harriet. Each hour brought new guilts to the surface of his thoughts. They stuck to his mind like flies to fly paper; he couldn't shake them. Obsessive thoughts, like rude little bugs nagged at him, relentless in their insistence.

He glanced at the table and noticed the green Gideon Bible neatly placed by the lamp. Strictly on impulse, he grabbed the phone and dialed the number before his nerve failed him. It was Anne's voice on the machine.

"You've reached the Martin residence. This is Anne. Sorry, but Tom and I are unable to answer your call at this time. Please leave a message after the tone...and have a nice day."

He cradled the receiver in defeat.

He snickered, remembering his childhood days of Sunday School pins and perfect attendance records. His head fell back on the spongy couch cushion; he stared at the ceiling while big, bright tears tumbled out of his eyes and rolled down his cheeks. He made no effort to stop or wipe them. His emotions were taking him for a ride; he hadn't paid the fare and didn't know the destination.

His mind went back to his childhood and the Sunday school class about the waywardness of King David, remembered his teacher's question and his answer.

"Even leaders, like kings, can make mistakes." She continued.

"And what was David's sin?"

He hadn't missed a beat. "He, ah, took another man's wife and then fixed it so's her husband would get killed in battle. I reckon he was a coward" he'd said.

He remembered how his classmates laughed and the trouble his teacher had had trying to restore order.

"And what did King David do?" she'd inquired of his younger self.

"He confessed his sin and the prophet told him God had forgiven him."

She thought that was very good of him to remember the gist of the Bible story.

His eyes gushed now and his insides began to convulse with grief and regret, guilt and shame. He folded in half and began to wail. From the inner recesses of his being, a cleansing flood came up and out, shaking him to the core. From a million miles away, the refrain of a song floated up from within. An off-key piano played it; a small town choir sang it.

"What can wash away my sin? Nothing but the blood of Jesus."

The song continued to spin in his head like cotton candy, turning and tumbling and soothing and promising...peace.

A stream of people paraded across his mind's eye now: aunts, uncles, brothers, cousins, old folks and children, all filed by and took their place at the "mourners bench," took their place to confess and resolve and receive a new life through that crimson flow. He reached for the Book and joined them now, prayed "the sinner's prayer," asking Jesus into his heart, hoping against hope that the childhood magic would work, now...for him. He closed the book and sighed in relief.

And fell sound asleep.

CHAPTER TWENTY-FIVE

Brant was nearing the end of his story. Harriet was a willing, captive audience. Had she not known and trusted her former husband, she wouldn't have believed a word of it. But she knew Donnie, and knew that one fault he didn't own was exaggeration.

"When I got back to my flat, I had a beer. Should have known better, but I didn't think. Some of Harley's boys had doctored it; I mean the lights went out, fast. Next thing I know, I'm in the middle of the bloomin' desert, left for dead; bloody maniac. I wouldn't be here now if one of them hadn't softened, like I told you. I owe him one."

"But what about the paper, Donnie, what about the deed?" Harriet insisted. What happened to it?"

Brant laughed.

"S'pose Harley thinks I've got it with me. Actually, I expect him to show up here. He'll he bloody surprised, old connivin' bastard."

"Donnie, why? Where is it?" she asked.

Brant looked carefully into her searching eyes, sighed, and then smiled like the proverbial cat that ate the canary.

"Left it with Willy. He gave it to Papa."

He leaned back in his chair and grinned from ear to ear.

A puzzled Harriet replied, "I don't understand. What will Papa do with it?"

He sat and stared at her for what seemed like the longest moment in recorded history before answering her with solemn finality.

"He went 'walk-about.' If he or that deed are ever heard from again, it'll be the surprise of the century."

Her mouth agape, she pressed him, "You mean he just did that Aboriginal 'disappearing act'...with the deed?!"

"Mean exactly that, Pet. The main thing is, the Aboriginals don't want the land now, anyway. The important thing to them is the honor of it...the government official's making good on his word. Now that Papa has that paper, the dying will stop."

"But how can you be so sure?" she asked.

"I trust Papa's assessment of the situation a lot more than some government authority's. Look, I love these people, always did. I never would have chased after that document in the first place if I didn't think it would help them to have it."

He folded his arms across his muscular chest firmly.

"Harley don't need to be makin' any money off of those people. And to hell with Conley and any other 'Pommie.' Fair's fair and that's it. I'm just glad the whole thing's over."

Harriet shook her head in disbelief.

"It's like some weird movie plot...really too fantastic to be real. If I didn't know you; I just can't work it out."

At this, they both began to undress for bed.

Brant sniffed, "Join the club, Pet."

She clicked her tongue as she responded, "And Papa's gone 'walk-about.'"

He walked slowly over and behind Harriet and began rubbing her shoulders. She turned to face him and they kissed.

"Harri, I'm sorry. Really...about everything. Do you think you can ever forgive me? Think we could somehow get back to 'square one?'"

She looked deeply into his eyes, hers filled with a new-found compassion.

"What's this? Getting mushy in your old age?"

Smiling, he said, "I'm not that old."

With that they resumed their embrace and kiss. He pulled her down onto the bed and looked down on her hopeful face.

"I'm serious, Harriet. This whole caper's been kind of a 'wake-up' call for me."

Pleading, she whispered, "Don't rush me."

"I won't" he said.

His story finished, they slept, looking for all the world like a happily married couple. The previous few hours had forged them together in a way no ceremony could. Talk was not cheap; it was priceless. A strange, new dimension had been added to their relationship. A missing "something" had entered, and like "psychic glue," had cemented their souls in a fresh and different union. Even their love-making had changed; it was softer, somehow.

* * * * * * *

Bonnington was only an hour away, and he would rudely interrupt Donnie's new relationship with Harriet. The former policeman followed the road with a determined stare, his headlights occasionally illuminating a wallaby whose eyes seemed to question the reason for his rude intrusion into its night. He was freshly fueled, still belching from the last shot he'd had for the evening. He rotated his neck, trying to work out the driving kinks, and turned up the radio. His mind whirled, trying to sort out the tangled mess of a case he'd been assigned to. Regardless of the "in's and out's," the bottom line was still Brant. The girl didn't have the deed; he doubted Brant's wife did. His answers waited in Kawanga. And he would be there before long: be there and be satisfied.

CHAPTER TWENTY-SIX

Lord Conley stood with his hands on his hips, facing the open safe in the wall, the small one, behind the impressionistic painting named *Eleanore*. Its emptiness mocked him, a glaring physical reminder of the all too real seriousness of the situation. A tingling sensation played at his spine and his groin. He stepped closer, looked deeper, breathed heavier, hoped harder, as though sheer force of will could somehow, magically, cause the dusty deed to materialize.

The safe remained stubbornly empty.

He slammed the door, slapped the wall and folded his thick arms over his rotund frame. He strained to give his neck freedom from the confines of his still too snug, tailor-made shirt. His arm felt strangely numb; his vision blurred and cleared again.

"If I could just get my breath," he thought, he would feel a lot better. "Damned shoddy tailoring," he fumed to himself. He stumbled over to the intercom and buzzed Anderson.

"Yes, Sir...what is it?" the voice queried.

"My pills, Anderson, my pills. I'm...I've got a bit of a problem. Come quickly."

"I'll be right there," the speaker replied.

Presently, the servant walked in on Conley leaning against the desk, struggling to get his bearings, endeavoring to steady his ponderous poundage. Anderson gave him the pill which the elderly statesman hurriedly put under his tongue.

"If I could just get me breath, a bit; damn shoddy tailoring!"

"Sir, if I may say, don't you think this might be related to the heart a bit more than to the stitch?"

"S'pose you're right, my man; but then, you're most often always right."

At this, Anderson spied the open safe.

"Something wrong over there, Sir?"

"Uh...no...the safe's quite all right; quite all right."

Smiling, satisfied, he inquired, "Will there be anything else, Sir?"

Conley coughed, straightened himself. "No, Anderson, that will be all. Thank you for the help...and the common sense."

The servant bowed slightly and exited the office, leaving the lord alone with his empty safe and emptier thoughts. The old gentleman again adjusted his collar, winced, looked up at the safe and sighed in defeat.

CHAPTER TWENTY-SEVEN

Camille and Harley rummaged through Brant's living room, beginning with the oriental rug. Finding nothing, they sat opposite each other on the floor.

Disgusted, Harley whined, "Well, guess our boy took off with the bloody deed. Ya know, I still can't believe he bought my story. How ya figger a guy like that, eh?"

Her eyes widened, "You're still convinced there's nothing to this? Nothing at all?"

"Completely convinced. But I can see you're not. What's it gonna take to get your mind off this?"

"My husband's got an awful lot of money. I'd say there's a never-ending supply just waiting to be tapped."

He pursed his lips.

"I'm not saying you're wrong. I'm just saying this isn't the way to get it, blackmail I mean; there's just nothing to this caper. It's a dead end."

Unconvinced, she added, "But why? Why would Brant go to all of this trouble for something that doesn't amount to anything?"

He shrugged his shoulders. "Who knows? Maybe he's got some bloody soft spot for the 'Abbos.' The simple fact is, he's wasting his time; let's don't waste ours."

Camille appeared intrigued but still skeptical. Harley took her by the shoulders and pulled her to himself, kissing her roughly. They tumbled onto the floor. As she came up for air, she queried him: "You wouldn't lie to me?"

Smiling broadly, he lied, "Me? Deceive a lovely lady like yourself? Never! Never in a million years and not for a million pounds."

She looked up at him, smiled and pulled him down to her as they resumed their kiss. He pulled back momentarily.

"Hey, what say we go back to my place. We'll get you settled and you can try and forget this whole thing and bloody Brant to boot?"

She smiled, nodded in agreement and they slowly got up from the floor.

Back in Harley's kitchen, he poured Camille a drink and slid it across the table to her. She took a long swallow and sighed in relief.

"Well, now, that's better, me lady, eh?"

She purred, "Mmmm, much. I think I could sleep for a month. Think I'll get a start on it right now."

The phone rang and she answered it, offering the receiver to Harley.

"It's for you; someone named, Bud. He says it's important."

Harley grabbed the phone from her.

"Yeah, this is Harley. What's up?"

Bud stood in the phone box at the back of the pub whispering into the phone.

"A couple of your mates told me you're lookin' for Donnie Brant. The way I gets it, there's some money for anybody who can put you on the right track."

Meanwhile, Camille yawned, got up and left the kitchen, making her way to the back bedroom. Harley watched her leave before answering Bud's question.

"Look, you're a bit late, Sport. The way I get it, Brant's gettin' a much needed suntan 'bout now. So what're you drivin' at?"

"Just this," he added, looking furtively from side to side. "I nosed around his old lady's place a bit, that's all."

Harley hugged the phone closer to his hairy ear.

"What's that s'posed to mean to me?"

"Just that I found somethin' there. Found a piece of paper,

that's all."

Harley's eyes widened.

"What kind of paper? Just what're you gettin' at?"

"What's in it for me?"

Exasperated, Harley sighed, "Look, there's enough to go around. You tell me what you found and I'll cut you in."

"Even share?"

"Even share; now spill it!"

"Not much to spill, Mate. Just one word...a town: Kawanga."

His face a mask of puzzlement, Harley croaked, "Kawanga?! That's an outback town. What the hell's in Kawanga?"

Bud chuckled. "Beats me black and blue, but I reckon ol' Brant is, since his ol' lady done left Sydney real quick-like for Kawanga already."

Camille's face was pressed against the door, listening intently to Harley's end of the conversation.

Harley responded, "Look, you bring two blokes with you and meet me there. When we finish with Brant, there'll be enough 'jack' for all of us. Think you can handle that?"

"No worries," Bud replied. "See you in Kawanga."

That said, he slammed the receiver back onto its cradle and barged out of the booth.

Harley hung up the phone and moved quietly to the bedroom door where he opened it quickly, surprising the eavesdropping Camille.

"Sleepwalking, pretty lady?"

"I, uh...I was thirsty...I thought I'd get another drink.

He smiled wickedly.

"There's more where that came from. Much more."

She smiled weakly, took the drink he offered and headed back toward the bedroom. Harley closed the door, looking away at the front entrance. Then he turned back toward the bedroom door and slowly opened it. He stood in the doorway, watching Camille drinking like she had the rest of her life to empty the glass. He strode in and took his place directly in front of her. Shocked, she dropped the glass, looking up at him, startled.

"You shouldn't oughta be listenin' in to other people's bidness."

She backed onto the bed without taking her eyes away from the rough man with the big hands.

"You really thought you could pull one one me, didn't you?"

He slipped around her in a fraction of a second and knelt on the bed, placing his meaty hands around her slim neck.

"I'm going to get the deed; I'm still going to blackmail Conley. I'm gonna bleed that pompous sow one 'pound' at a time."

He tightened his grip.

"Wait," she gasped. "We could...."

"Could what?" he interrupted, looking off into space, vacantly. "Share the money? Sail off into the sunset...live happily every after?"

She struggled in vain to somehow free herself from her rude assailant.

"Just give me a chance...I can help...I can...."

Pursing his lips with grim resolve he cut her off.

"You can die, me pretty: quietly. You can be a nice little loose end, all tied up in a pretty bow."

He squeezed tighter. Camille's eyes bulged, her breath failed. Harley smiled, closing his eyes.

* * * * * * *

Harley sat on the sand now, hat cocked on the back of his head, pants legs rolled up to his knobby knees. He squinted in the moonlight as his eyes scanned the deserted section of the beach before him. He scratched his scraggly chin and took a long swig of whiskey from the bottle beside him, hoisted it in the air in a mock 'toast' to Camille.

"To you, Babe," he croaked. "May you rest in peace, wherever the hell you are. You was quite a ride, you was. Damn straight you was pretty; I didn't lie 'bout that."

He took another long pull from the bottle.

"But...what do they say? 'Pretty is as pretty does?' An' you sure didn't do pretty, did ya? No, you didn't, Camille. An' if you was lookin' for a relationship...." He waved his hand in disgust. "Then you was as crazy as you was beautiful."

He looked vacantly out into the sparkling water. "I live my life just a step above them fish out there you're sleepin' with. He slowly stood up on the shore, wobbled, tossed the bottle into the water, paused and took off his hat.

He threw it into the water also.

* * * * * * *

Harley was obsessed.

Nothing and no one would keep him from the deed and the money it would bring him.

One by one, he had eliminated anyone who might oppose or accuse him. Brant hadn't had the paper; he'd been left to die in the desert, out beyond the outback. His last resort was a bit of information one of his hired mates had picked up while searching Harriet's apartment for the deed; it was an enigmatic little word: Kawanga.

He would be in the god-forsaken excuse for a town in an hour or so. He and three of his "friends"—expendable ones—would soon discover the location of the prized possession. They would find it and with it make Harley rich beyond any of his previous schemes.

He had planned long enough; now it was time to do something to achieve his goal, to bring his design to fruition. What had begun as a tiny thought-speck in his mind had grown and developed into a full-blown scenario that would have made any screenwriter jealous: a script complete with intrigue...and murder.

Harley's Jeep rumbled along on its way to Kawanga. Meanwhile, Bud and his partner were jostled back and forth by the rough terrain and the truck's ancient suspension as they, too, began their approach toward the same destination.

Bud's partner asked, "You reckon ol' Harley's gonna make good on the dough?"

Bud replied, "Damn straight he will. I don't do no 'freebies.' If he tries to stiff me, I'll slit his throat."

"Too right," the man replied with a grin. "We'll give 'im a smile from ear to bloody ear: startin' with 'is wrinkled neck!"

"Maybe that's what we oughta do anyways...," Bud concurred.

"Goodonya, Mate."

The truck sped by, becoming a distant speck on the road.

* * * * * * *

Harley peered through the windscreen, a determined look on his weathered face. He took a long pull from the whiskey flask beside him, burped, licked his lips and sneered at the road ahead. He muttered to himself, "You still alive, eh Karate-boy? I'm gonna put you to sleep: permanently!" He wiped the whiskey from his lips, straightened his hat and took a firmer grip on the wheel.

Adrenaline shot through his bloodstream as his headlights lit the sign announcing sixty kilometers to Kawanga. He was beginning to taste the upcoming confrontation. Maybe there was more to it than just retrieving the missing deed. Maybe it was also a chance to recover a fading manliness, to rediscover an athletic prowess in a final confrontation with Brant. Yes, he'd had an uneasiness—call it seaman's intuition—about Brant's still being alive, even after seeing to it that the brothers wouldn't live to collect their share of any blackmail money. He forced his shoulders back and inhaled deeply of the night air. He would make good all the way. He would be a hero, an adventurer, something more than a retired sailor, filling a pub stool, babbling to other drunks some archaic drivel of the sea.

He tightened his grip on the wheel, picked up the flask and "toasted" the windscreen.

"Bloody Brant, I'm comin' fer ya!"

CHAPTER TWENTY-EIGHT

Brant slept quietly beside Harriet. Presently he winced, moaning in his sleep, as the familiar dream took shape yet again. A young Donald watched his drunken father threaten his mother in a familiar shouting match. He listened to his mother exclaim, "Stop shouting! Must you always shout so?" His father countered with, "I'll do worse than shout! I reckon I'll bust yer snot-box for ya!"

Brant's boyhood persona sprang from the table, jumped between his parents and grabbed and twisted his father's upraised hand. He spun and threw his father to the ground, leaving the drunken sot unconscious. His mother, sobbing, ran to him, hugging him to her bosom in gratitude. He heard her plaintive question, "Oh, Donnie...when's it gonna stop? And what would I do without you?"

He gently patted her shoulder, his expression concerned and wistful.

Brant's face contorted as he awoke, startled, from the dream. Stunned, perspiring, he sighed and lay back down to get his bearings. He looked over at Harriet, sleeping peacefully beside him. He looked up at the ceiling, his eyes following a crack in it to the wall mirror across the room displaying his reflection. Awakened from his reverie, he stretched and clasped his hands behind his head. There was no way out of the town before Harley, or Bonnington for that matter, would get to him. He could feel their approach; his fighting instinct assured him he was still their prey. They were both, for different reasons, ruthless hunters.

In a way, it seemed to make sense, that it should end like this, with Brant more than likely fighting for his life. He lay there with his eyes open, watching the sunrise through the dirty window. Harriet's back was to him; she was still asleep. He reasoned and remembered his best defense would be a formidable offense. He determined to initiate the combat. If he was to fight, it would be on his terms and his turf.

He bolted out of bed, dressed and left the room before Harriet had even turned over. Brant briskly walked two miles out of the town to the reservoir. He passed the placid place and made his way to the dirt road just outside of the edge of town. The sun had just risen, streaking the sky with red and yellow. The air was still; he knew he had to be as quiet, centered, as poised as he had ever been for any competition. He was not fighting for a trophy; he was fighting for his life.

Brant was clad in a well-worn "gi" a uniform in which he had sweat and strained his way to the top of the tournament circuit. The frayed black belt sported four soiled strips of off-white electrical tape, signifying twenty years of dedication to the oriental fighting art. His bare feet carried him determinedly forward, away from the hotel, toward the reservoir, over a mile from the town. Brant, perspiring, his well-muscled chest protruding from the half-open uniform, had an almost emotionless expression. He squinted in the approaching sunlight and continued walking.

* * * * * * *

Harley's Jeep sat at the edge of the road. Presently, the pickup truck arrived and parked beside him, engine idling.

Bud asked, "Where's the guest of honor?"

Harley rumbled in response, "If he is still alive, I reckon he's between here and the town; can't be but a few miles. Tom left the bugger in the desert but I've driven all through the area on the way here. He must have nine lives."

Another of his partners added, "Think he's gonna wish he

was a bleedin' cat when we find 'im, eh Harley?"

The old man put his hands on his hips and nodded.

"Leave your heap here," Harley growled. "Climb in the Jeep and let's get on with it. I got a pile o' money to collect and I ain't getting' any younger!"

The two men sprang out of the truck and into Harley's vehicle. It sped off down the road, toward the reservoir, toward Kawanga.

* * * * * * *

Donald Brant took his place in the very center of the gravel excuse for a road, feet folded in front of him, in "meditation position." Birds soared overhead, plants and animals began to stir to life as day began. His palms were open, the backs of his hands resting on his knees. With his eyes closed, he breathed in, slowly, through his nostrils and exhaled, deliberately, through slightly parted lips. With each breath a deeper calmness settled upon him. In a few moments, the past and future dissolved into the present moment.

Brant sat there, suspended in space, one with the sun and sand and sounds of the morning.

In the distance the rumble of a four-wheel drive automobile could be heard, interrupting the tranquility of the moment. He opened his eyes and examined the surroundings. The terrain was barren, except for an occasional "ghost-gum tree," a stark, white-barked reminder of a former time of life. The bleached trees had no foliage; some of their barren limbs narrowed into points like bony fingers of death: botanical skeletons.

The Jeep was in view now, carrying four opponents, rough and ready individuals, fired by the promise of an almost limitless supply of money.

The vehicle rolled up to within twelve feet of Brant; the engine idled, then chugged to a stop.

Harley leaned back in his seat and spoke quietly out of the side of his mouth to the three sweaty men he'd hired to incapacitate his enemy.

"There's our man, boys. Bloody athlete, he is. He's still dressin' in his pajamas." He laughed. "Let's give him a nice, long sleep to go with, eh?"

The men chuckled and disembarked, standing just in front of the Jeep.

Harley raised his voice and called over the windscreen.

"Looks like you need lessons in how to die, Sport. Thought the Yank left you to get a nice tan a few days ago."

Brant slowly got up and straightened himself to his full height. He stood there, tanned and toned, squinting in the sunlight.

"Look, Mate, I know why you're here and you're wasting your time. I don't have it."

He folded his arms in front of him, over his waist and the dangling black belt.

"No, reckon you probably don't," Harley laughed. "But your wife, now there's a more likely proposition. Matter of fact, me and the boys here, we're on our way into town to...'talk' to her 'bout that, right now." He smiled broadly in the morning sun.

"She's out of this. She's not in town; left last night. She's a couple a hundred miles away by now" he lied. He returned the smile.

Harley's faded into a steely determination.

"Where is it?" he demanded.

"Let's just say it's in a safe place. Yeah, it's in the safest possible place...under the circumstances."

He put his hands on his hips.

"Now why don't you and the 'girls' get back in the truck and go find yourselves a beer, eh?"

Harley's men folded their hands into tight, balled fists and began to move toward Brant, one directly in front of him, one to each side.

"You know, I'm no good at all to you dead," said Brant, his voice even with his emotions.

Harley barked, "Got no plans to kill you, Sport; I'd have brought armed men if I'd had that in mind. We just plan to 'persuade' you to give us the address of that little piece of paper."

He nodded his men forward.

"It's too bloody hot for this, but, what the hell," sighed Brant as he readied himself for the conflict.

The one in front, the short one, lunged forward with a round-house right punch. Donnie moved back and then slid the man's arm over and down with the inside of his left foot, executing a textbook crescent kick. As his opponent bent forward, his face was met by Brant's right foot, as he followed the move with a jump front kick. The little man lay face down in the sand.

The other two looked at the man on the ground, then at each other, then at Harley, then at Brant. They gritted their teeth and rushed at him, attempting to put out the martial fire with their combined weight. There was a dull thud as the men collided and collapsed. Brant yelled and stomped his heels on each of their necks. The entire confrontation had lasted under three minutes.

Harley was gone, making his way to the reservoir. Brant wiped the sweat from his forehead with his forearm. He took off after Harley and caught up with him at the little wooden dock.

"Look, Gramps, let's just forget this," he shouted. "I told you, there's no way on this earth you'll ever find that deed. Fact is, the 'Aboriginal's' have it. Gave it to an old one, father of a tribe; and he's gone 'walk-about.'"

"Walk-about!" Harley shouted.

"You bloody bastard. I will kill you after all; dirty sonuv-abitch." He lunged at Brant who stepped back as Harley landed on the creaky boards.

The floored man grabbed a piece of tackling and lashed at Brant as he spun towards him. Donnie reared back, blood pouring from the gash in his middle. He rolled to one side as the old sailor swung again, the metal fingers grasping the rotten wood flooring. Brant was behind him now choking Harley.

"Let it go," Brant grunted, sweat pouring from his face.

Harley drove his left elbow into Brant's mid-section, opening the wound wider. Then he ran from the reservoir, back towards the road. Brant reeled with pain, tore off his uniform top and stumbled after him. Harley was crawling into the back of the Jeep just as Brant grabbed his shoulders. He pulled the old man out and around.

Brant was looking into a gun barrel.

Harley wiped his mouth with his shirtsleeve.

"No reason to keep you alive now, Sport. No reason at all. You're no good to me alive; and you're no good to me dead. Fact is, I like the idea of you dead a bit better, 'bout now."

He cocked the trigger, aimed at Brant's chest.

"There's no way out of this for you, Harley. People in town, they're gonna trace all of this to you. Harri will see to that. She's back at the hotel now...waiting for me."

"No. Think you'll be waitin' for her...in hell. Then I'll arrange for her to meet you; one more isn't going to matter now. There's nothing left for me now, anyway; nothin' at all."

For a split second, Harley looked away as one of the felled men moaned. Brant rushed him and whacked the gun loose from his hand. Harley drove his crusty boot into Brant's stomach sending him backwards into the gravel and sand. He rolled over as Harley dove toward him. Harley scrambled to his knees and came at Brant's stomach with his head. Donnie brought his knee up to meet the old man's pate. He stumbled and punched Brant down with a strong right fist. The old man stumbled backwards, shaking the cobwebs out of his head. Brant rested on his elbows in the sunlight. He took a deep breath, got up and ran towards his opponent, who was still dazed. He shouted as he launched a flying side kick that caught Harley under the chin. The old man was airborne for an instant. A moment later he landed, impaled on a dry branch of a "ghost-gum." The end of the limb protruded from his middle, looking for all the world like an Aboriginal "bone." Brant gasped at the eerie sight.

Harley was barely conscious. He looked up at Brant with a pained question on his face. He died trying to utter it.

Brant tightened his belt as the shiny, blue Commodore drove up. An elderly ex-cop stopped the engine and got out of the car.

Brant stood with his hands on his hips, the sun beating down on the two of them.

"'Fraid you're a bit late, Mate."

"So it seems," said Bonnington, looking at Harley.

CHAPTER TWENTY-NINE

It was cooler inside the phone box. He closed the door behind him and rested his head against the glass. He let out a sigh, exhaling disappointment and discouragement, depression and despair. He had to tell him; Conley had to be informed.

He grasped the receiver with a loose fist; he stood there, drained, waiting for the operator to finish making the connections. His eyes were empty, mirroring his soul. The bartender, busy with his glasses, glanced over and saw this shell of an ex-policeman, this living corpse, engaged in his conversation with the other side of the world.

"It's over, Sir, all over," he lamented.

"And the deed, you have the deed?"

"No, Sir; I don't," Bonnington replied, eying the bar. "I'm afraid no one has it, not Harley, not Brant, not Camille; no one."

The fat man's heart began to race; perspiration burst from every pore of his body. Immediately, absentmindedly, he began to fumble with his necktie, opening his top button. His breathing was labored, his arm was going numb.

"What in hell are you talking about?" he shouted. "What's that supposed to mean to me, 'no one has it'?"

"What it *means* is that Brant gave the bloody document to an Aboriginal medicine man, a shaman. That's it; that's the lot, full stop, Sir."

He dropped his head, glanced at his shoes, looked up again, his words and thoughts empty. He stood there, glancing at the bar, running his tongue back and forth along his upper lip.

"Damn it, Bonnington, get it! Find the bloody 'Abbo', and bring it back. What the bloody hell do you think I've been paying you for?"

Conley's breath was coming harder now, his chest felt imprisoned beneath a weight much heavier than his.

"'Fraid that's not possible, Lord Conley. Thing is," he coughed. "Thing is, he's gone 'walk-about': disappeared, gone."

He waited for a reply that never came.

Conley dropped the receiver and began tearing at his shirt collar. His vision blurred as the pain intensified. A million pounds had been dropped on his breastbone. He toppled backward, slammed into the desk and slid to the floor. He lay there on the shiny, marble tiles looking up at the polished, ornate ceiling. The bookcases leaned over, as though intrigued, peering at his curious predicament. In his mind's eye he saw a black cave. He watched as the hut came ever closer, finally into full view. He saw a withered, weather-beaten old man, heard him chanting, mumbling words in a foreign tongue. The hand filled his whole field of vision; now, a thin, white bone stared him in the face. He watched it until it faded...away.

Bonnington hung up the phone.

He opened the door and closed it behind him, shutting out the conversation and the retirement hopes that had motivated him for the past few weeks. He sauntered over to the bar and took his seat; it was warm, waiting for him.

"What'll it be, Mate?" asked the jovial man behind the counter.

The weary, weather-beaten detective put his elbows on the bar, his chin in his right hand. He thought for a long moment and then looked the man square in the eyes.

"You tell me."

CHAPTER THIRTY

Brant reached for the blue sky above him and took one long, leisurely stretch. He surveyed the horizon and smiled at the gulls swooping and sailing over Manly beach. The whole scene spoke of peace, relief and a return to the calmer, happier life he had known before his life's course had been altered by a musty, dusty sheet of paper in an obscure, British vault. He sat, cross-legged, in the hot, white sand, the wind blowing his thin, blond hair away from his face.

The fresh ocean air was agreeing with Harriet. She lay on the blanket in a trance, hypnotized by the sound of the surf. She was intact. The experience had left her wiser, more self-aware, more committed to restoring her marriage than she could have ever thought possible. She half-sat up, leaning on her elbow.

"Well, what do you think, Mr. Brant?" she smiled. "Shall we give it a go, again?"

He replied while continuing to look off into the distance. "Yeah, why not, eh?"

He turned to face her and laughed.

"Oh, you," she said, pushing him back onto the beach towel.

She leaned over him and looked into his squinting eyes.

He waited a moment before he said, "Listen, Harri; you're the best thing that's ever happened to me. If this whole business has taught me anything, it's taught me that. I blew it—us—before; I can't let that happen again, Pet."

She looked up and away at the waves, feeling the spray against her cheeks. Harriet turned and looked at Donald again and said, "We'll see, Luv; we'll see."

   She leaned back on her palms as the breeze caressed her face. The two of them looked like a postcard. He covered his face with his rolled up shirt as the white light of the afternoon sun drained the last bit of tension from him.

ABOUT THE AUTHOR

JACK HALLIDAY enjoys wide and varied interests. At various times he has been a musician, horse trainer, martial arts instructor, radio and television broadcaster, hypnotherapist, published author, optioned screenwriter, and world traveler. He has been a contest finalist, and his work has appeared under various pen names in *Hardboiled Magazine*, *Taekwondo Times Magazine*, *Horse and Rider Magazine*, and others. Several of his nonfiction books have been translated into other languages. He lives with his wife in the Midwest.

ABOUT THE AUTHOR

JACK HALLIDAY enjoys wide and varied interests. At various times he has been a musician, horse trainer, martial arts instructor, radio and television broadcaster, hypnotherapist, published author, optioned screenwriter, and world traveler. He has been a contest finalist, and his work has appeared under various pen names in *Hardboiled Magazine*, *Taekwondo Times Magazine*, *Horse and Rider Magazine*, and others. Several of his nonfiction books have been translated into other languages. He lives with his wife in the Midwest.

SWAN SONG

AND OTHER
MYSTERY STORIES

JACK HALLIDAY

THE BORGO PRESS
MMXII

SWAN SONG

Copyright © 2012 by Jack Halliday
"Moonlight and Roses" was originally published
in *Hardboiled Magazine* #44 (February, 2012).

FIRST EDITION

Published by Wildside Press LLC

www.wildsidebooks.com

DEDICATION

In memory of Howard Browne

"Imitation is the sincerest form of flattery."

CONTENTS

SWAN SONG

"The phrase 'swan song' is a reference to an ancient belief that the Mute Swan (*Cygnus olor*) is completely mute during its lifetime until the moment just before it dies, when it sings one beautiful song."—*Wikipedia*

"The silver Swan, who living had no Note,
when Death approached, unlocked her silent throat.
Leaning her breast against the reedy shore,
thus sang her first and last, and sang no more:
'Farewell, all joys! O Death, come close mine eyes!
'More Geese than Swans now live, more Fools than
    Wise'."

—Orlando Gibbons

CHAPTER ONE

I left Hal's office at about four-thirty.

As I made my way down the hall, I got to thinking about what we'd discussed: the script and the changes he thought it needed before anyone would buy. I was disgusted. I felt like someone had taken the salt off my popcorn. I nudged the door to the men's room open and stood next to a short, balding guy in his late seventy's. I felt sorry for the poor devil as he stood there, looking at the ceiling, then down at the urinal, waiting.

"Bend your knees," I said as I zipped up my pants.

"'Xcuse me?" he peeped. I smiled and spoke louder.

"Bend your knees; it'll start the flow."

He smiled as the stream began. "I'll be damned," he said.

"Hope not," I replied as I dried my hands. He hadn't heard me.

I went out and stood in the hallway, leaned on the sill and looked out over the city.

"What do I do now?" I asked myself.

It seemed as if I were all alone, a spectator of life rather than a participator in it. Maybe that's why I'd become a writer, to seal myself off from actively participating in the "veil of tears" ordinary folks seemed trapped and tripped by. My reverie was interrupted by a nudge in my ribs. It was the old man.

"Thanks, fella," he smiled. "I'll be damned," he mumbled as he shuffled down the hallway toward the elevators. I sniffed in amusement and thought about how easy life would be if all of its problems could be solved as simply as dealing with a kink in the prostate.

The moon was bright when I got home. It felt like some celestial being was following me with a huge spotlight. I decided to have some coffee out on the back porch. The air was still and cool as death. I sipped and stared and drifted off into that semiconscious state between wakefulness and sleep. And that's when it hit me. I had nowhere to go and nothing to do, at least for a week. Why not head out to who knows where and see what life is all about anyway? Hal's rewrites could wait at least that long; I was still flush from my last sale. It was definitely a writer's thing to do. I could blame it on "writer's block."

Before my logical mind could interrupt, I threw some clothes and toiletries into a small, leather bag and tossed them into the back of my Wrangler. It surprised me how fast I got on the interstate. I looked up into that cloudless night and the moon smiled back at me.

I guess I'd driven about two hours when an all-night diner's lights winked at me in the distance. I was mesmerized and pulled into the lot. I slipped out of the car, stretched and then sauntered into the little beanery. What met my eyes looked like it'd come out of one of my screenplays. A few grizzled, old fellas sat at a few gnarled, old tables sipping Joe and mumbling about whatever folks in this town had in common. I took a seat at the counter as the waitress turned to face me, dishrag in hand, lipstick in place, hair not.

"What'll it be?" she smiled. One gold tooth sparkled in punctuation. I put on my best poker face and asked for coffee and two donuts. She put her hands on her hips and just stood there, smiling and staring as I sugared and creamed my coffee. My looking up at her didn't faze her or her smile.

"Haven't seen you in here before; just passin' through, huh?" she asked.

Before I could answer, there was a loud bang outside, followed by gravel spraying and a muffler announcing the departure of a hit and run driver.

"Holy hell," one of the old guys shouted. He looked up and over at us with his mouth agape, eyes wide and coffee running down his chin. "Holy hell," he reiterated. "Somebody's Jeep just got kissed." He was looking at me now.

She clicked her tongue and I spun off the stool and quickly made my way outside. There was my Wrangler, all right, hit so hard it'd done a 360-degree circle. I looked at it carefully and sighed in relief that it hadn't been ransacked at all, just pushed against its will, hard. I leaned against the driver's side door with my arms crossed over my chest. It might've been funny if it wasn't so inconvenient.

"Pretty bad?" she asked from the doorway.

I turned around and smiled weakly and shrugged my shoulders. "Don't guess I can get anything done about this till tomorrow, right?"

"Jim—he's the local mechanic—doesn't work nights, 'specially after midnight. We gotta room though, if you wanna wait. Otherwise, a bus'll be along in about an hour. Next town's about ninety miles away." She raised her eyebrows slightly and pursed her lips.

"You look like it's your fault," I laughed.

"I think everything's my fault," she replied. "C'mon back inside; you haven't touched your donuts."

I hadn't.

I felt better back in the diner with the hot coffee inside me. It had started to drop cold outside.

"Well?" she asked.

"Oh, the room. Sure, why not; I'd love to spend the night here," I lied.

She smiled victoriously and rested her forearms on the counter in front of me. She looked up with her eyebrows raised expectantly. "You gotta name?"

I smiled and answered between bites of stale donut, "Chip; my friends call me Chip. That's what you can call me. And what should I call you?"

"Audrey."

I downed the bean and set the cup in the saucer. I was trying to figure out which of my characters I should slip into to get me through this evening. She motioned with her head.

"C'mon; I'll show you the room." Audrey threw a towel over her shoulder and swayed her way from behind the counter.

"You need a porch for that swing," I heard myself think.

The room was at the end of the hall. It was a quaint little affair: bed, chair, desk—complete with mirror sporting the mandatory crack in the upper right corner—and dresser. I remember her showing me the bathroom and beginning to wonder if there was any way she came with the room. It wasn't long after, that I blacked out.

I couldn't get my eyes open. I felt like they belonged to someone else. Every bone in my body ached as though I'd gone twelve rounds with Roy Jones, Jr. I wished I were Roy *Rogers*, hightailing it out o' Dodge on ol' Trigger. But I wasn't. I was a beaten up screenwriter who couldn't get his eyes to obey his scrambled brain. A century later one lid fluttered open, just a little. A wave of nausea hit me and I closed it. Then I tried again, this time with both eyelids in unison. It was like bringing a video camera into focus. I couldn't move my legs; at least it felt like I couldn't. But I finally did, with great difficulty. I was in a praying position, the room still threatening to spill me back on my backside. Slowly, I steadied myself enough to crawl over to the window. Some kind of annoying insects made an annoying noise in the distance (I don't care for bugs). I peered out into the night and saw Audrey talking to a chunk of granite wearing a cowboy hat. She threw her head back and laughed at the moon while Granite put his hands on his hips and chuckled enough to make his belly shake "like a bowlful of jelly." If he were Santa Claus, I'd happily skip Christmas this year.

"This isn't fiction," I reminded myself, cold fingers of fear tickling my groin and spine. "What the hell has happened to me?" I asked myself in the quiet of the room. I would have gladly kicked myself in the tail for being so stupid, but it would've hurt too much. *Billy the Kid* was leaving now. I couldn't help but notice the ding in his left front fender. Even one of the *Three Stooges* would have spotted the red paint from my car on it. Audrey was still smiling, arms folded across her copious bosom. It hadn't registered before, but she was a beautiful woman in her own way. Long, curly blonde hair, a wasp waist and tan, muscular legs. Even clad in her apron, you could tell she was "fit as a fiddle" and ready to set up the first B-movie writer to pass through town past midnight.

"If Hal could see me now," I lamented.

I wondered why; "Why pick me out of the mob of faceless humanity?" But then I answered myself, "Why not?"

I was a bit startled to hear the door creak. I braced myself for the worst when I saw my uninvited guest was a young boy. He looked to be eight or nine years old and could have doubled for "the Beav," even down to the freckles on his rounded cheeks.

"Shhh," he said, his finger poised against his lips. "I'm not s'pposed to be here."

"Neither am I," I replied, sliding away from the window and bracing my back against the wall. "And who might you be?"

"My name's Sammy. That's my mom outside. She has a gold

tooth."

"You don't say."

"I reckon it's worth a pile o' money."

"I reckon," I agreed. "Hey, how about you telling me what you're doing here?"

"I came ta see how you was; heard the slammin' around, you know."

"No doubt."

"Are you okay?" he asked.

"I reckon," I answered. I was getting a bit bored with our conversation, not to mention the fact that it sounded to me like he was speaking into a barrel.

"What's your name?" he asked with a Cleaver squint.

"Chip Delaney...let me save you another question. I write movies, though I doubt that you've seen any of them."

"I gotta coupla ideas for movies."

"Get in line," I mumbled.

"'Scuse me?" he asked.

"Never mind," I sighed. I struggled to sit up against the wall; my eyebrows furrowed as I attempted to keep the little twerp in focus.

"So, isn't it a bit late for you to be up?"

"Yeah, that's why I'm tellin' ya to keep it down. If my mom finds out I'm still up, she'll kill me."

I looked out of the window again at an empty parking lot, the lone lamp barely illuminating it.

"What do we do now?" I asked the little wise guy.

"I'm goin' back to bed; that's what."

"Sounds like a plan," I smiled weakly.

With that, he whisked out of the room, closing the door behind him.

I shook my head in disbelief and rested against the wall. This was definitely the first "whammy" in this picture (that's a movie term for a startling incident that should happen in an action film about every ten minutes or so). The door creaked open again. I could see trim ankles walking toward me by the moonlight streaming into the room. One of them sported an anklet with little, silver hearts dangling from it. "This lady is some piece o' work," I mused. She was looking down at me now, her eyes widening, her mouth opening, her hand coming up to her lips to stifle a scream I interrupted.

"You oughta be in pictures," I sneered.

"Chip; Chip, my god, what's happened to you?" She crouched down beside me and put one strong forearm under each of my armpits and started getting me on my feet before I could begin to protest.

"What on earth...?"

"You took the words right outta my mouth."

I slumped into the chair and she stood in front of me with her hands on her hips. "You don't think I had anything to do with this?" She appeared genuinely shocked at the suggestion I hadn't yet vocalized. "I was outside...."

"Laughing it up with Buffalo Bill," I interjected.

She clicked her tongue. "He's my ex; Sammy's dad."

"We've met."

She squinted at me. "You know Rick?"

"I know Sammy; but don't tell him I told you. He's supposed to be asleep."

She clicked her tongue again and shook her head in disappointed amazement. "That boy."

"He's a cute little guy," I said as I massaged the back of my head. "You should have a dozen of 'em."

She sniffed and smiled, "He's one of a kind, Sammy is."

She sat down on the bed, across from me. As bad as I felt, I was getting ideas.

"You have children?" she asked.

"Only the kind that come out of a computer."

"What?" she asked, her gold tooth bouncing a sparkle back at the moonlight.

"I'm a screenwriter. To me, writing movie scripts is like having a baby, only they don't take nine months."

"I like that," she smiled.

"How 'bout morning sickness?" she continued.

"Can't say that's ever happened either, though I have had unusual cravings at odd hours; like *Yukon Jack* and *Twinkies* at three a.m."

"I've got both of 'em downstairs in the kitchen," she smiled.

"Great; let's have a pajama party. I'll wait here while you get the goodies," I said weakly.

"You sure?" She slowly stood up, the moonlight catching her calves.

"Definitely."

"Well, I'd better go downstairs then and get started on our party," she whispered.

"I'll be here; it's the only game in town," I replied with a shrug of my shoulders. I winced as I did that. She stood in the doorway momentarily.

"Is there something I can do about your bumps and bruises?" she asked.

"Nothing comes to mind at the moment. Although I can't say that won't change by the time you come back upstairs."

She ran her tongue over her top lip, opened her mouth to say something, thought the better of it and disappeared into the hall. I listened to her heels clicking their way down the rickety steps. I asked myself what had happened and got no satisfactory answers. It was depressing and exhilarating at the same time. I decided to go with exhilarating.

It was then that I started really trying to put things together. With any luck, I could be out of this 'burg in a few days. No point in filing a complaint of any kind; the authorities would only side with the "local" anyway. No, just wait it out, take my chances with the mechanic of choice and get this episode behind me. "Hey, maybe there's a movie in this somewhere," I consoled myself. "Maybe not."

I looked over my shoulder through the window at the moon. I wondered if the cow would be jumping any time soon. Before I could reply to my musing I heard the steps creaking again. Something like *Rive Gauche* preceded Audrey. Apparently, I wasn't the only one getting ideas. The moonlight caught her hair as she bent over the table, setting down the glasses, bottle and box of *Twinkies*. She looked up, put her hands on her hips again (apparently her seductive pose of choice) and smiled triumphantly.

"Well, here we are. All the fixings for a late-night treat. Want some?"

Slowly, I got my feet under me and straightened up to my nearly six feet height. The minute I started wobbling, I rested my back against the wall.

"You know, you look a lot like that karate guy on television, the one that played the Texas ranger, only younger and without the beard."

"Don't I wish I had his money. As a matter of fact, I'd settle for selling him a script."

She patted the bed beside her.

"C'mon, sit down and have a snack and a little fun with me."

I sat down and had a snack with her.

And a little fun.

CHAPTER TWO

"Why did you do this?" she asked. She had propped herself up on the pillows, her back against the headboard. I couldn't believe she was actually smoking a cigarette. I bit my lip, refusing to ask, "Was it good for you?"

"I suppose I could ask you the same question."

"That's simple; I'm lonely and you're the first guy in years I've had the least inclination to get close to, physically or otherwise."

"What about Rick?" I asked.

She sniffed in disgust and mashed out the cigarette in the chipped ashtray on the nightstand next to her. "To hell with Rick."

I thought I saw you laughing it up with him out in the parking lot last night."

She turned toward me and leaned on her elbow. She squinted and shook her head. Audrey turned away and looked at her feet poking out from the bottom of the blankets.

"Well," I continued.

"Well, what?" she asked.

"What's the story with 'Man Mountain Dean?'"

"Rick is...was a mistake; the only good thing to come out of us was Sammy."

I was getting a little concerned about her dodging my questions. I lay there thinking for a moment. Then it occurred to me, "What's the difference what her relationship is with whomever? It's got nothing to do with me; nothing at all."

I slid my feet over and let them dangle off the edge of the bed. The air was cool and my mind was suddenly clearer. I didn't even feel particularly sore. Maybe that Canadian whiskey had done the trick. Or maybe it was the *Twinkies*. Or the combination. Or maybe it was Audrey. Right on cue, she leaned over and whispered in my ear. "Was it good for you?"

"When do you think that mechanic you mentioned might get around to looking at my car?" I asked.

"I'd say early morning. He's not that busy this time o' year and I bet he'd welcome the chance to work on a four-wheel job like yours.

"So, was it good for you?"

I just looked at the black of night through that dirty window. She gave up and threw on her clothes. "It's been awhile, but I don't remember ever getting any complaints," she added.

"Well, then I guess your record's perfect," I replied with a smile. All I could smell was her perfume. She smiled.

She checked the time as she put on her watch. "Hey, I gotta get downstairs and think about opening up. What about you?"

"Me? I never open up on the first date."

She frowned.

"I guess I'll stop over and see what Jim can do about my wrinkled Wrangler."

"He's good; if it can be fixed, Jim can fix it."

Somehow I wasn't convinced, but no real alternatives came to mind either. She turned and looked at me from the doorway.

"I guess you'll be takin' off right after, huh?"

"Guess so, yeah." She nodded her head and left the room, closing the door behind her.

I dressed and sat on the edge of the bed, thinking. No, more like watching my thoughts parade past my inner eyes like a video on fast forward. When I pressed the stop button I was still as confused as I was when the movie started. "This guy's writing is worse than mine," I lamented to myself. And that's when that tingling started again; the hair on my forearms stood at attention. There was something just too convenient about all of this. I wondered about Rick and Sammy and Audrey and Chip Delaney. How did they all fit together? And for how long? And why? There was a faint tapping on the door.

It was Beaver.

"You comin' down for breakfast?" he asked with that Cleaver squint.

I looked over my shoulder at him. "Is it any good?"

"Mom'll make pancakes if somebody besides me wants 'em."

I turned around and lay on my side on the bed with my head propped up in my hand. "And you'd like me to help you out, is that it?" He nodded, smiling.

"Tell her I want three big ones, with sausage on the side and a bottomless cup of coffee."

"If there's no bottom, how ya gonna drink it?" he asked.

"And orange juice; tell her a large orange juice."

"You wanna a bottom on that?"

"Definitely."

His eyebrows scrunched together as he thought about that for a moment. Then he smiled broadly like he'd just thought of something fantastic.

"My mom's got a gold tooth."

"So you said."

"I did?" He seemed genuinely surprised.

"You did." He shrugged his shoulders and pivoted, slamming the door behind him. I winced and plopped back on the sagging mattress again. I interlaced my fingers behind my head as I wondered about just what I had gotten myself into.

CHAPTER THREE

Breakfast was better than I had anticipated. Audrey was a good cook. She seemed to be good at a lot of things. Like setting up a hack writer from the Midwest maybe? But for what? And why?

While I was considering these questions the door opened and the ever-interesting Rick entered. He looked like a slightly red sausage wrapped in a flannel shirt and overalls. For the life of me I couldn't figure Audrey with him. He nodded, grunted and plopped down on the stool at the other end of the counter.

Sammy's eyes widened impishly as he looked at Rick, then at me and finally at his mother. If I didn't know any better I'd wonder if he were trying to decide if Sausage and I were planning on coming to blows over his golden-haired mother. I had no such ideas. I just wanted out of this town and quickly. But that would depend on the local mechanic's expertise.

The room was oddly silent; the breakfast crowd—such as it was—hadn't arrived yet. I was beginning to miss my apartment, and my computer, and a body without bumps and bruises received for no logically apparent reason. Rick looked over his left shoulder at me, sniffed in disdain and watched himself in the mirror drinking coffee. I was watching Audrey in the same mirror. If she were involved somehow, she was a much better actress than a lot of the has-beens that got cast in my films. It was embarrassing, really, getting clobbered and not knowing who or what to blame.

"Think Jim will have any news about my car?" I asked her.

She looked over her left shoulder, head tilted, blonde curls dancing on the lapel of her pink uniform. It occurred to me she looked for all the world like Anne Francis in *Honey West.*

"I'd say there's a good chance, yeah," she smiled.

Rick sniffed again, tilted his coffee mug way back, drained the cup and slammed it on the counter hard enough to cause the silverware to shuffle. He slid off the stool, tried in vain to hike his britches up over his paunch, settled for a mile or two below his navel and slapped a bill over his check.

"Later," he grunted to no one in particular.

Meanwhile, Sammy was trying to make the remains of his pancakes a permanent part of his plate by mashing them circularly with a gooey thumb. Apparently, you got more power going if you stuck your chin out during the procedure. Poking your tongue out of the corner of your mouth didn't damage the process either, I noticed.

"Sammy; stop playing with your food," Audrey barked.

She stood facing him, hands on her full hips, her one ankle behind the other, the one sporting the anklet with the little hearts. I was really expecting a director to holler "Cut" at any moment on this production. But this was bizarrely real. Surreal, even.

Her little freckle-faced urchin thrust a big red lower lip out at his creation, then looked up and smiled that television-star smile. She beamed and looked at me.

"Isn't he something?" she asked. I looked over at the little squirt and nodded my approval.

"He is at that."

And I felt my heart go out toward him...and her.

It was a bit overcast and gloomy when I made my way over to the garage. I was greeted by the smell of grit and grime, ancient oil spills and soiled rags and what-not. Dust a few feet thick blanketed the makeshift table just inside the door. The area served as a combination waiting room and office. A 1978 calendar—complete with girly photo—greeted me as I entered and looked through the window at my Jeep. It seemed kind of sad, almost like it was winking weakly at me, the left headlight squeezed into an unnatural shape. Jim was looking up from under a sports car job that was on the lift. I tapped the window a few times and he finally brought his sandy-colored head out from under the car. He nodded, gave me a "one second" with his index finger and pulled a soiled cloth from his overall pocket, wiping his hands as he made his way to the employee entrance at the other end. I didn't like him. Maybe it was his one artificial eye, but he had a menacing look about him, like a "heavy" in one of my action scripts.

"So, you here about the Wrangler?" he asked, cocking one hip as though he were auditioning me for a small part as a lug nut or wrench.

"I am," I replied, ignoring his belligerent affect.

"Can't say when she'll be done. Need a coupla parts that ain't so easy to come by; you wit' me?" he asked, squinting, his plastic eye continuing its interrogating gaze.

"Now, why doesn't that surprise me," I muttered.

"'Scuse me?" he whined.

"A couple days, you think?" I responded, again ignoring his question and attitude.

"A couple, a few, what's the diff, right?"

His smile was about as genuine as the creamer in the can on the beat-up desk beside him. He shuffled through some papers and pulled out what looked like an invoice. He shoved it toward me, a cracked *Bic* pen between his dirty thumb and the smudged paper attached to the clipboard.

"Just sign the bottom. That there authorizes me to work on her."

I scribbled my name illegibly and threw the whole affair on the desk.

"I'll be staying over at the diner," I said as I turned to leave.

"Audrey's place," he said to my back.

I closed the door behind me without responding.

Women are funny. In a lot of ways. Mainly, they're generally inclined to nearly insist that you "open up" and really share your soul with them or they're certain you're not really being "authentic." The funny part comes in after you decide to throw caution to the wind and open up your self or what-ever the little guy inside is called and then they carve him up in time for Thanksgiving dinner. Oh, and did I mention that that's just about the time you realize they never did open up their heart? By then of course they've gone on to butcher some other unsuspecting lug while you're left trying to piece together what's left of dinner. The oftener this happens, the less there is left of Humpty. And then all of those jagged edges left over begin to impinge on others you're less intimate with. Makes for a more detached experience of life. After all, why injure inno-cent people?

It was about six o'clock when I tried calling Hal on my cell phone. Naturally there was no service. I seriously doubted there ever would be in a town like this. I could imagine the telephone lines getting organized and initiating a boycott—anything—to keep their monopoly on the communication in and out of this place. In some ways this town seemed like a resident of a retire-ment community. From a distance it appeared quaint and harm-less, almost intriguing. But up close and personal you ran into the stale smell of Old Spice and cheap whiskey and war stories and what's wrong with the world and all that. There was some-thing wrong here, something uncomfortably unsettling. It made me wonder if Stephen King were somehow involved.

I was lying on the bed, my hands behind my head, watching the streetlights come on. I drifted back to my childhood, remem-bered my bedroom and another window looking out on another streetlight, felt the earphone in my ear and my fingers fiddling with the dial on that crystal radio set my old man had bought me. I was gonna become an electrician like him. A blue collar wonder-boy with a real family and a mortgage to prove it. That was before it all fell apart. A rap on my door whisked me back to the present.

"Feel like something to eat?" Audrey asked, hopefulness lighting up her cobalt blue eyes.

"Jim says it'll be a few days before that car of mine is road-worthy." Her brows furrowed and she pulled a face with her ruby red lower lip thrown into a pout. Then the sun rose as she smiled.

"Guess you're stuck with us for awhile then."

"Seems like it," I sighed, then returned her smile. "Come here." She crossed her arms over her bosom and cocked her beautiful head to one side.

"What's in it for me?" she asked, squinting narrowly with one eye.

"You won't have to cook," I replied.

CHAPTER FOUR

She was gone when I awoke. The phone rang. The odd part was no one knew I was here except the locals. And why would they bother to use the phone when they could talk to me face to face in a matter of minutes? I lifted the receiver off of the cradle and waited. Nothing but breathing. Then a cough. Then nothing.

This was really starting to become annoying. Thank God the headache had all but disappeared and the bumps and bruises were settling down considerably. But this bizarre little town continued to play its squirrely games with me. I was actually starting to wonder if one of my writer friends hadn't somehow gotten wind of my little impromptu trip and arranged this madness just to jerk my chain. In my heart I knew that scenario wasn't even remotely possible. I starting thinking about leaving the car and just getting a bus back into town. Then the phone rang. Again. No voice, just breathing followed by a coughing fit and then silence. I lay back down and fell back asleep.

I had a strange and frightening dream. I was in the bottom of a stainless steel shaft, highly polished, its walls impossible to scale. As I lay there, suddenly a beautiful face, framed by blonde curls peeked over the edge. The voice echoed as it bounced back and forth between the walls. "Chip, Chip" it yelled. The third time I heard my name called I woke up with a start looking into

Audrey's striking face. I hadn't noticed the number of freckles across her nose and cheeks before. Between them, her golden skin, shockingly blue, almost purple eyes and blonde hair, she didn't need any makeup at all...not that it stopped her from trying to improve on nature's gifts. Even her breath was captivating, like something between honeysuckle and mint. I spotted a freckle on her lip and kissed it.

"You were snoring something fierce. Sounded like a band saw working its way through treated wood."

"I must've really needed the rest."

She leaned back, turned her head slightly, frowned.

"Are you okay?" she asked.

"Right as rain, I reckon," I answered as I righted myself on the bed, throwing my legs over the side. I rubbed my hands over the spread and found it beginning to feel familiar. That couldn't be good.

"What's up with your car?"

"Lean, mean, one-eyed Jim says he needs a bit more time with my little Jeep."

"I'll bet it's a parts problem," she sighed.

"Most things are," I muttered.

"What's that supposed to mean?" she asked, wrinkling her perfectly maintained eyebrows.

"Listen," I said. "There's something a little bit odd about what's been happening here. I mean, I just wanted to get away for a little while to clear my head and maybe get an idea for a new screenplay and I wind up here, beat up and without my car in working order. I'm just starting to wonder, what gives?"

She sniffed, looked out the window and then turned those dark gleaming orbs back in my direction. "So you're trying to figure out a polite way to 'dump the broad with the kid,' eh; and just when things were getting interesting."

"No," I countered. "It's not that. I don't know what it is; that's exactly the problem. With a script, you start with the end at the beginning." Her brows bunched.

"What's the best part of a joke?" I asked.

"The punch line, of course," she replied smiling but still confused.

"Well, it's the same with writing," I replied. "You simply figure out your destination before you begin and then 'write backwards'." She raised those lovely brows now.

"If you say so; you're the writer. Me? I'm just the hired hand."

"And what beautiful hands they are," I said, grasping them firmly in mine. She lowered her head and stared deeply into my eyes like she was examining the very last vertebrae in my sacrum.

"I like you, Chip; a lot. I haven't felt like this about anyone in a very long while. I know we just met and I know it might seem corny and clichéd, but it's still the absolute truth. Why does everything have to mean something?"

I sighed and pulled my hands away, lay back on the bed with my palms behind my head. I said to the ceiling, "I'm just not comfortable with the accident and the paint on your ex's car matching the smears on my Jeep." She shook her head and answered the window.

"Why would Rick smash into your car? What would he have to gain? What would he get out of it?" She turned back as I responded.

"That's what I can't figure; but I aim to and the quicker the better for me. I'm not saying I don't have some strong feelings for you either, Audrey. But what kind of relationship, what type of new start could we have if he's somehow mixed up in this?" At this she stood up, hands on her hips, again facing the window.

"Rick," she said, clicking her tongue. "Always Rick. Just around long enough to make a mess for me."

"Audrey," I cut in. She raised one hand.

"It's okay, Chip; it's happened before and plenty of times." And with that she left the room, closing the door behind her.

CHAPTER FIVE

It was the rumble of what sounded like a diesel engine and tires slowly spinning away on gravel that grabbed me out of my sleep. I slid out of bed and made my way over to the window. Pulling the dusty drapes to one side I peered out at the street below. Audrey was taking some bags from what looked like a twelve year old girl: the spitting image of her, only in miniature.

"What next?" I asked myself.

All eyes were on me as I made my way downstairs and into the diner. Some of the locals nodded and I smiled artificially striding quickly to a table in the corner. From that vantage point I could see the entire restaurant—such as it was—as well as the entrance and a fair stretch of the road leading out of town. Smoke from the garage's chimney across the street reminded me that my Wrangler was still awaiting it's operation at the hands of the local Dr. Jekyll. Actually, I expected to run into Mr. Hyde at any minute. Things had been screwy enough so far.

The *Rive Gauche* brought my eyes back to the inside of the room and Audrey asked, "And what would the world's greatest screenwriter like this morning?"

"About last night," I started. She wrinkled her nose.

"Let's just stick to the menu, shall we?" she said. I put my chin in my hand.

"What does the management recommend?" She pursed her lips, narrowed her eyes and a smile slowly came from back-stage.

"How about blueberry pancakes with a side of turkey sausage?"

"Turkey for the 'turkey' sounds about right to me," I said, returning the smile. She smiled knowingly.

"We'll have time to talk about the 'other' later," she said with finality.

"You're the boss," I replied as I leaned back in my chair.

"Now that would be a change of pace," she answered with

her back to me. I sniffed at the thought of her being pushed around by that chunk of lard for longer than she deserved.

Suddenly my eyes were drawn to the stairs. "Little Audrey" slowly made her way down the rickety steps, smiled weakly at the patrons whom all seemed to avert her eyes, and then took a seat at the counter. Her daughter had the saddest eyes I had ever seen in a young person. I couldn't help but wonder what her problem was.

Audrey began talking something over with her but I couldn't make it out. It was none of my business anyway. Or was it? Then the young girl looked furtively in the mirror and right in my direction. I assumed Audrey had told her the "Cliff's notes" version of our meeting and relationship. She shrugged her shoulders, looked at her mom and then back at me. With another shrug she took a long drink of her orange juice. I shook my head in consternation and looked out the window again, using my right palm for a chin rest. First the "Beav" and now his older sister. Not to mention their mom. Nature had ushered me into a ready-made family. It seemed like it was happening all over again. But I'd sworn off any and all serious relationships a long time ago.

I drifted off into a reverie that took me back a number of years—more than I like to admit—to a small liberal arts college. And to Marilyn. I know, I know; a teacher is absolutely not supposed to fraternize romantically with the young ladies under his charge. It should be Macbeth and not Lolita, but tell that to the hormones and unfulfilled longings of a middle-aged professor.

Funny, but it wasn't the physical dimension I remembered at all. It was the walk around the reservoir at twilight with a breath of mist in the air. And listening to her read her latest short story to me, blonde hair all done up in a ballerina braid, oval face rising out of a blue turtleneck sweater, sky-blue eyes flashing with the excitement that only comes from the opening of the psyche to allow the real writer's voice to speak its first faltering phrases. The girl was so doggone beautiful she literally stopped traffic one evening as we walked arm in arm through a congested downtown at the tail end of rush hour. I remembered one guy in particular, shocked out of his stare at her by the rude awakening of the of the driver behind him leaning on his horn. The poor schmuck's expression seemed to communicate it was a small price to pay for a few seconds more of a lingering gaze at her. I felt embarrassed for him and beyond delighted for me. I wanted to tell him, "Yes, she's real."

The smell of coffee in front of me brought me back into the present.

"Where were you?" Audrey asked, tongue firmly in cheek.

"Long ago and far away I guess."

"Well, see if this food doesn't keep you tethered to your chair for a while, okay?" she smiled.

"Absolutely," I said.

"Hey, who does the young lady at the counter belong to?" Audrey smoothed her apron, folded her arms over her chest and smiled in sweet satisfaction.

"Gloria is the pride of my life," she replied, looking at the thin, pale blonde whose back was to us. She looked around, made her decision and sat down across from me.

"I thought you said Sammy was...."

"I did," she interrupted. "Gloria was the result of one of many one night stands. I am thoroughly ashamed to say I really don't know who her father is. I've told her he was a childhood sweetheart named Larry who died in the Vietnam war before she was born. She's okay with that, has been at least up until now."

"She is the spitting image of you," I replied. She nodded.

"Everyone says so. Just wish she'd inherited some of my toughness. Funny isn't it? How we can wish with all of our might that some things just weren't so and yet it doesn't seem to matter."

"How so?" I asked. Audrey pursed her lips, breathed out and then continued.

"Gloria's had a...rough time of it. She's been away for almost a year...in a psychiatric facility."

"What happened?" I asked as I began to work on my breakfast.

"Not really sure. The doctors put it down to some sort of traumatic experience but I'll be darned if I can come up with anything. They say she suffers from some kind of 'critical incident stress disorder.'"

"What's the treatment been so far?"

"Why?" she asked. "You looking for a new script idea?"

"No, not at all," I continued. "I've done some study in that area, a long while ago; I used to teach."

"Really?" She looked genuinely shocked.

"What, can't a guy have more than one interest at a time?"

"Of course; it's just that you don't seem like the type to probe into somebody's soul, invited or not."

"You'd be surprised," I countered.

"I'll just bet I would," she replied. "Hey, I better get back to checking on the others here or I'll have to consider firing myself."

"Wouldn't that be a shame." I smiled.

She got up, patted my arm and began her table by table inspection, filling coffee cups as she went. My eyes met Gloria's again in the mirror. Maybe it was my imagination but I was almost sure a flash of flirtation appeared for the briefest fraction of a second. It shocked and saddened me with a startling intensity. Jerking my eyes away I felt my old friend "the tingler" making his rounds from my groin, up my spine and into my reddening cheeks. What had I gotten myself into?

"Hope springs eternal," or so says the poet. I never really bought that. It always seemed more to me like depression was the constant confidant. Never really figured out why that gray shadow seemed always just a few inches or feet away. Remembered as a kid, during a thunderstorm, feeling like the world was ending. I can still smell the freshly painted back porch stairs, that pale blue color, just a shade lighter than the sky. I looked way up where God is supposed to be and shuddered as the heavens rumbled and the lightning flashed, started

crying without thinking about it, sucking my thumb as my mother suddenly appeared and tried to comfort me.

"It's just rain, Chippy; just rain. God's crying over some of His children who're having a tough time. It'll stop; just wait a few minutes." And it did, but that somber pall remained.

It was there when I was just a bit older too. I was on the floor in the kitchen playing with some toys while my mother was fixing dinner. My old man walked in the back door and came over to her and gave her a hug. I looked up and he seemed to be about ten feet tall. Suddenly I wanted him to pick me up and hug me more than I'd ever wanted anything in my entire little life. I was afraid to ask him. He looked down and smiled. Then my old friend, the "gray cloud" returned. I don't remember what happened after that. All these years later I wonder how my life might have turned out differently had I asked him for that hug. "Big doors open with little keys," someone once said. The door had remained locked for me all these years. Tried different combinations but never came up with the winning one so I'd settled for something much less. Much less.

CHAPTER SIX

It was later that afternoon when it hit me to ask Audrey out on a "date." Fortunately for me the diner closed early on Wednesdays so she accepted without even a mock hesitation. Gloria could take care of the little guy and that would leave us alone for the afternoon. I'd seen what looked like a large park or cemetery on the way into town. Maybe I was trying to get in touch with some long lost roots but I just envisioned a picnic there. Audrey was all for the idea so we slipped out a few hours before sundown with basket and bottles in tow. I felt my pulse quicken as I followed her up a trail. We'd left her little Toyota back on the street where it could mind its own business while we minded ours.

Something started thumping in my neck in time with the

flexing of her very muscular calves as we continued to make our way deeper into the woods. Turns out it wasn't a cemetery but a former burial area; former like when the Indians used to put their dead to rest in the presence of the Great Spirit. I was glad when we reached the clearing. She had no sooner spread the blanket she'd had tucked under her freckled arm when I spun her around and kissed her so hard I felt her teeth, then something else, wet and warm. The kiss ended and we just looked at each other. She was out of breath and her eyes were clouded over. I suppose mine were too.

"Where'd that come from?" she asked, hands on her full hips.

"From a raging sea of hormones, I reckon." I grinned. I set the basket down and we both sat, Indian-style, her back resting against a large, aged tree, mine braced against my arms behind me, hands spread out on the cool, dark soil. Time stood still. A very soft breeze came through, rustling leaves and depositing an absolutely unearthly quiet. I nearly cried; it was so peaceful.

"What's wrong?" she asked, her perfect nose slightly wrinkled. I kicked a pebble, looked at her.

"Not an absolute thing I can think of." She smiled.

"You've done this before."

"What, kicked a stone in the presence of a beautiful woman?" I laughed.

"Who was she?"

I shook my head sheepishly, looked down at the ground.

"A student of mine. I had planned a picnic, very much like this one. But it never happened."

"Student?" she asked, puzzled.

"I mentioned before I was a teacher, too many years ago. Well...." Audrey put her hand up in a policeman's "stop" signal.

"Don't tell me; you got involved with some little coed." I reddened as I shook my head with embarrassment.

"Not actually 'involved, sexually,' but still a little too close for academic comfort, I'm afraid."

"What happened?"

"She transferred; left, period."

She looked off into the distance, then turned those beautiful eyes back to mine. "I'm not a coed; never darkened a school door past high school."

"And I'm not interested in your higher education."

"What *are* you interested in?"

She tilted her lovely head without breaking eye contact. She was so attractive, so open and inviting, so trusting and yet independently strong at the same time that I felt she must have been in Eden. I reached for her and took her face in my trembling hands. I wanted to have this woman with me always. I brought her face closer to mine, dizzy with the smell of her perfume. Her mouth was inches from mine. I heard the breath leaving her nostrils, watched it drift over the tiniest pale hairs above her ruby red upper lip. I placed my cheek against hers; we breathed in unison.

Then a shot rang out that shattered the moment like a red brick smashing through a window. We threw ourselves on the damp ground simultaneously. Wide-eyed, she started to scream but I quickly covered her lips with my index finger. Her scream died unborn and she lay there, chest heaving. Ever so slowly, I sat up in the ensuing quiet that was replacing the chaos of a just a moment ago. She propped herself up on her elbows.

"Hunters?" I asked, trying to minimize the madness.

"You know, it's funny, but I suppose it could be," she answered, relieved at the possibility.

I was not as encouraged, not at all. The car wreck, the sandbagging at the diner, the strange phone calls and now this. It was a puzzle all right, but where were the pieces? There was no board to even lay them out on. None of this made any remote, logical sense.

So far as I knew, no one even knew where I was, let alone why I was here.

My photograph had never graced the walls of a post office and I even paid my parking tickets on time. Sure, some unsuspecting ham'n'egger might've *wanted* to kill me after renting one of my epics, based on the DVD'S box art only to find out what a stinker the picture really was, but to actually follow through on the urge?

I seriously doubted it.

"Whoever or whatever it was seems to be gone," she said. I nodded in agreement. I looked around at the surrounding greenery and sighed in frustration.

"What?" she asked.

"That's exactly what I'm asking myself," I replied.

We rolled up the blanket and took the basket back to the car. I lowered the trunk lid and looked into her eyes. They appeared as innocent as her little boy's.

"What?" she asked again.

"I was just thinking maybe I should take a bus into that 'next town' you told me was only about ninety miles away."

"What for?" she asked, a little animation spreading into her cheeks.

"It's not anything about us," I said, attempting to reassure her. "I just feel like I need to get off dead center. I was thinking if I could check some things out on a computer, maybe in a local library, I could start to make some sense of all this, find some sort of a clue as to what could be going on." I opened the passenger side door for her. She got in and looked up at me with the lost look of her daughter.

"You could borrow my car."

I closed the door, went around back and got in my side. In a few moments we were back at the diner. I reached over, opened her door and she grabbed her purse and got out. She spun around quickly and bent over, looking at me from the window.

"Might as well take the food with you. At least one of us should have a little something special to eat."

I sniffed with chagrin.

"Thanks, Audrey. You are one in a million. Seriously, you're worth your weight in gold, so keep eating!"

She waved me off and I drove away watching her in the rear view mirror. As if on cue, she placed her hands on those marvelous hips and got smaller and smaller as I drove out of town.

A large white sign done up in cursive lettering spelling *"Welcome to Belleville"* greeted me as I eased the car into town. I was reminded of Rod Serling's favorite *Twilight Zone* episode, "A Stop at Willoughby." I doubted if *"Mr. Misrel"* would be waiting on me for the conference call however.

It was sunny and almost peaceful after I parked the car and made my way down the sidewalk to the large, gray stone edifice engraved with the words, *"Belleville Library"* over its doorway. The various passersby looked as though they had traveled from the fifties just to be with me...so I wouldn't feel out of place; it didn't matter to them that I wasn't even born in that decade.

As soon as I entered the building I was engulfed in warm musty air that surrounded me like a blanket. I punched the elevator button and looked at the four walls of the inside of the lift as you always do and waited for the *"ding"* and the open doors and the walls and walls of books ready, willing and able to take me anywhere their authors decided.

There were only a few patrons on this floor and a lone librarian seated at a desk viewing something intently on her computer screen. She looked to be in her late sixty's and reminded me of Lily Tomlin with a little more meat on her bones and minus the sense of humor.

"Can I help you?" she asked as she looked up at me through gold-rimmed glasses, smoothing her bangs away from them.

"Just wondered if I might borrow a computer for a coupla minutes," I replied with my best engaging smile.

"Of course," she said as she spun around and out of her chair. She had quite a caboose for her age and job. I wondered how Audrey was doing.

I followed her to the work station, seated myself and enjoyed her perfume as she leaned over my shoulder—closer than necessary—and showed me the ropes. "Used to be automatic time limits on these but they've been disabled. We welcome visitors nowadays. No use in discouraging them from staying, right?" I smiled artificially and nodded as I logged on and into my AOL account and listened to her heels click their way on the linoleum floor back to her desk.

The computer screen seemed bright and cheery like an old friend.

I went through my emails. There was nothing special, certainly nothing threatening, nothing unusual at all. Only some more notes from Hal about my script. He knew where he could put those notes. He wasn't a bad guy really, just seemed to be a little more demanding lately. He had a nice stable of clients: writers, directors and actors, and had been in the biz for over thirty years. I was really fortunate to have him. Unlike the average mid-size agency reps, he actively pushed my little literary efforts. I'm what you might call a niche screenwriter.

Hollywood's a small town and if you have the right connections and a real "voice," no matter how raspy or rusty, a decent agent can keep you busy writing B pictures for the cable and international markets. I'd initially interested him through a little novella I'd written and self-published with one of his acting clients in mind. Turned out the actor loved the book so I took Hal's advice and turned it into a screenplay. It never sold but the ensuing dozen or so had and I finally had a job I could do in my pajamas. Even with "notes" and deadlines and rewrites, it was a lot less stressful than some other jobs I've held.

I checked the other two email accounts I had and turned up a great big nothing. What I needed was "Mike Hammer" but he didn't seem to be available and I couldn't have afforded him anyway. I logged off and made my way over to an arm chair facing a large window framed by ancient drapes of a nondescript color. As I looked out over the town square and its green grass, suburban population and easygoing ambiance I drifted off into another reverie.

I was back in high school. In the library. Waiting and watching for what new prank some of the guys were going to play on our eight-foot tall librarian. He was known to one and all behind his very large and bony back as "Lurch." While he wasn't really a member of the "Adams Family" he would have made a passable double for the original butler. I still felt bad for the old guy and what we'd put him through. He'd had a genuine love of and passion for books and learning but I don't remember him successfully passing them on to any of us. Maybe my own unhealed wounds made me more aware of the ones others carry.

That got me thinking about Gloria, Audrey's daughter. The more I considered things, the more I became convinced that she really had been flirting with me in the diner's mirror. Why had she needed psychiatric help at such a young age? Out of the blue I thought of Jim the mechanic. Wondered if he'd by any chance gotten a little too close for her psychological comfort. I knew quite a bit about childhood sexual abuse, both from reading and from serving as a school counselor at some of the colleges I'd taught at. Depending upon the extent and the emotional resilience—or lack thereof—of a young person, one or more incidents could be emotionally devastating. The so-called "one third rule" came to mind. The idea is, there are three kinds of responses to childhood or even adult trauma. The first is the person who undergoes a significant psychological shock and seemingly shrugs it off. After a time they're almost completely back to normal. The second individual is more seriously impacted. They generally require counseling and/or some sort of pharmaceutical assistance and in time they live reasonably well managed lives.

Then there is the third victim. They are permanently scarred and seared emotionally, psychologically and even spiritually. They never really recover and if they do manage to continue living even a semi-normal psychological life, they are not "all there," emotionally-speaking, and don't really live, but just kind of exist in an empty-shell type of world.

I thought about Gloria again. And wondered if I'd be able to help her. If anyone would.

It was time I got back to town so I retraced my steps, taking my time exiting the building. The sun was just thinking about setting as I slid behind Audrey's wheel and adjusted the rear view mirror. For a split second I thought I saw someone duck into a store front shop. That familiar icy feeling made its way up my spine pausing briefly for a little "do-se-do" at the base of my neck to give the hair on it a little needed exercise and then skipped to my fingers adding some perspiration to my palms.

Then I started the engine, jerked the wheel and got out o' "Dodge."

CHAPTER SEVEN

It was dark when I arrived back at the diner. The town seemed unusually quiet, even for this 'burg, and I noticed a lone light in the garage across the street. I guess you just don't click with some folks, but this Jim guy rubbed me the wrong way and vigorously. I decided to check on my car, not that I really expected any information or cooperation from him. Sure enough, he was at his makeshift desk scribbling on some work order or other. He looked up as I entered, the light gleaming off his artificial eye.

"Here 'bout yer car?" he asked with a squint.

"Just thought I'd check on the progress before I turn in for the night."

"Well, whoever it was done smashed into her done a real nice job o' messin' things up, inside and out."

"How much longer?" I asked, feeling that irritability rising up and demanding some notice from me. He leaned back in the creaky swivel chair and folded his bony arms over his soiled work shirt. He smelled too, and not from working on cars. The odor reminded me of a decaying animal.

"Oh, I expect I kin have 'er in some kinda workin' order in a day or so. Though I doubt she'll look jest exactly like she did before the big bang," he said with a bit of a cackle in his voice. His cheeks wrinkled like a dried prune as he let fly with his version of a smile. He was a first class creep all right.

"Ya know, when a car takes a big hit like yours did, why they's jest never the same," he winked. "It just messes with everything. Why, I seen folks jest up and dump their vehicle onced it was damaged like that. Ya git me?"

I was only too sure I "got" him all right. And I wasn't thinking about my car.

"I'll be back around in a day or so," I answered with resigned annoyance.

"That'll do nicely and I'll give ya a real 'Christian price' on her too."

I spun on my heels and left the garage vaguely aware of him chuckling to himself. He was the country bumpkin but the joke was apparently on me.

It was dark and quiet as I made my way up the stairs to my room. I'd stopped half way back to town to snack on the lost lunch Audrey'd left with me so I wasn't particularly hungry. As I quietly opened my door so as not to wake anyone, I heard something from the kid's room. It was muffled but I was certain I heard the little twerp's voice. I entered my room but stood in the doorway, the door open a crack.

"No, get off o' me!" he was saying. "Get off!" he repeated. That was followed by a "thump," then the sound of some clothes rustling. Gloria pushed open the door and grunted "Baby!" over her shoulder as she tiptoed her way down the hall, her pale nightgown trailing behind her. The door slammed shut and I could only imagine what Sammy was doing now. Getting to sleep eventually I hoped, but with what kind of nightmares waiting for him behind his closed eyelids?

It was no use trying to get to sleep. There was nothing doing on that score. I just lay there, my fingers interlocked behind my head on the pillow, alternately staring at the ceiling and off into the distance where the moon shone on the sleepy town. The familiar pall was just beginning to hover over me when I forced my thoughts into memory mode.

I was back home in my own bed after finishing my shift at the theater.

Those were the days all right.

"Captain of the ushers" I was, with the significant pay bump from seventy five cents to a whole buck per hour. It was break time and I stashed my work sport coat—complete with theater insignia—into the makeshift locker room and changed into my spring jacket. Seemed like I could actually see the traffic and smell the exhaust as I rushed down fifth avenue to the White House restaurant. It must be over thirty years ago now but I've never had a burger to beat theirs since.

I forced my eyes to remain closed so I could savor every innocent moment of the memory. The blast of heat and smell of onions cooking slapped me in the face as I quickly entered the place and grabbed one of the stools at the counter. The restaurant was all done up "retro style" only not by design. It was just that old. The joint was so crowded you could barely get your elbows up on the counter to try and drink your water or sip your coffee.

Quick as a wink she came over. At about thirty-two, she was at least twice my age but what a doll she was. Tipping the scales at no more than a hundred ten pounds, she couldn't have been any taller than five foot three or so. Her red hair and bright blue eyes looked like they'd been ordered as a "special two-for." She always seemed genuinely overjoyed to see me. Always, I got the conversation around to how her baby was doing and was there any news on a possible reconciliation with the low-life she'd tied up with.

I bolted upright in bed as I remembered the harsh restaurant light glitter off a gold tooth in her very pretty mouth as she smiled at me. Then I resumed my reverie.

We would talk as she wiped down the counter, refilled glasses and cups and generally straightened up her station. She was shocked and awed when I told her what I planned to do with my life after I graduated from college. She encouraged me to keep in touch but we both knew we wouldn't. I couldn't help wondering where that single mom was now as I lay here in bed in this strange little town in the middle of a moonlit night, alone in a room owned by her in a new incarnation.

Maybe there was something to that philosophy. A spiritual

"do over," a cosmic "control z" for those of us who managed to mismanage things the first time around.

I seriously doubted it.

When I got up the next morning I felt like I'd been "born again." I leaned over and retrieved the book that comes with every hotel, motel, or in this case, diner room. I was reading when Audrey walked in.

She looked like she'd taken a bath in sunlight. Her eyes seemed to be electronically lit from within. It was really quite shocking. Even her freckles seemed to be doing a synchronized dance across her perfect nose. Maybe it was the light flooding the room but I never fully realized just how classically beautiful she really was. For a moment I started to think I might actually belong here.

"Whatcha readin'?" she asked with an impish smile.

Her voice was always pitched lower than I remembered it and was just a bit raspy. I assumed it was the result of years of smoking. In any case it was just one more of her captivating traits. I knew so little about her, actually, and yet I seemed to know her totally. Perhaps I was having another mid-life something or other. At this stage in this very unusual game we'd been playing I really didn't care. I was just happy to be on board. Whether or not I'd ever get off this ride, or what condition I'd find myself in, if and when I did, was beginning to matter less and less the longer I was around her.

"I said, what's that you have there?"

She jerked the book from my hands, slapped it shut and threw it back on the bed. She plopped down near the foot board and curled one muscular calf under her very beautiful thigh, leaving her uniform slightly in disarray.

"You getting religion?"

"Wouldn't you be surprised?"

"I went to Sunday school religiously—no pun intended—all through my childhood."

"You don't say," I replied as I sat upright against the head board. She nodded with pride.

"Even got perfect attendance pins."

I mock bowed in admiration.

Her smile waned as she turned her pretty head to face the open window, the limp curtains moving softly in rhythm with an early morning zephyr.

"That seems like a lifetime ago," she said with a full dose of regret in her voice.

"How so?"

"How so?" She turned back to face me. Some of the sun inside her had gone down now, replaced by a shadow she had lived with for too long a time.

"I've told you I sort of lived my young adult life in the 'fast lane.' Actually, it was more of a moral autobahn. I guess once you're off and up to full emotional speed you just can't slow down. It's all too painful. The turns become too difficult to negotiate and you almost dare yourself to live faster, love looser, give easier, just to see how far out of control your life can really become."

One glistening tear made its way up and onto her eyelid.

"Oh, Chip," she sighed. "I've messed everything up. And it's all my fault—you don't have to remind me of that—I take full responsibility, for Gloria, for Rick, for Sammy, for everything."

Without thinking, I "signed the Cross" at her and said, "I absolve you from your sins in the Name of the Father, and of the Son and of the Holy Spirit."

She sniffed and smiled and I joined her in a little chuckle.

"Come over here," I said as I reached for her and she slid toward me. She rested against my chest and I stroked her blonde head.

"Maybe I need a dose of that ol' time religion'," she said as she looked up at me.

"Maybe we all do."

CHAPTER EIGHT

It had been almost a week since I'd started out on this impromptu adventure. So far it seemed to be the "fates" "10" and Chip "0." There was no player rearrangement to be done either. It had all been random, painful, life-changing, frightening and delightful.

But still the nagging wondering. And this latest business even involving a gun. Did I really believe the craziness at our ill-fated picnic could be a simple hunting misadventure? Dick Cheney couldn't have pulled that off. The very idea was ridiculous, even to a screenwriter of my questionable literary ilk.

No, there was definitely something underhanded and dangerous going on and I was apparently the target.

But why?

No matter from which end I examined the various facts, no adequate or even halfway sensible solution presented itself. That familiar tingle began to rev its little engine as the next few thoughts got into the queue. If I left this town when my car was ready, if I left Audrey and her kids behind and resumed what was, by comparison, my normal life, would the madness really stop?

I didn't believe it.

That's when I really began to accept the fact that I was under the scrutiny of person or persons unknown with an equally unfathomable agenda involving the hurt and/or eventual demise of my person.

For the life of me I couldn't come up with even a remote candidate for "stalker of the month." I simply wasn't that important to any person or for any reason. Sure, I'd held a lot of different jobs in my forty plus years on this whirling globe, but I always tended to blend in, to stay in the background, to seemingly survive any awkward encounter relatively unnoticed and unscathed by people and events that would trap and tangle others on the work force. That agility with anonymity was really one of the main reasons I chose my latest profession. Writing enabled me to live life vicariously and from a safe and sane distance. I could triumph through some of my characters and suffer in the skins of others. Either way, I was never directly involved. At least not until now.

Until Audrey.

I was just cleaning up my room, such as it was, when I heard a soft tap on my door. "Come on in" I replied as I folded a shirt and placed it back in the old wooden drawer. I turned to see Gloria standing there in the doorway. She was wearing a shirt-waist dress and I wondered how the current fashion trends had missed her. But then I remembered how she'd been away in a hospital for the last little while and what kind of a "blast from the past" this town was.

"What's your name?"

"Chip; Chip Delaney. Would you like to come in?"

She shrugged, then closed the door and sat down at the desk, folding her slim arms over herself.

"And you're Gloria, Audrey's daughter."

She nodded.

"My dad died in the war, the Vietnam war. He got medals."

"So I've heard. And what about you? Do you have any medals?"

She sniffed, quickly turned her head away and looked intently out the window as if she were expecting a UFO to land. Presently, she turned back to face me with an impudent look.

"Do you?"

I laughed, pushed the drawer closed and sat on the edge of the bed.

"Medals? Me? No; but I have a few scars."

Her eyes brightened.

"Really? Where? I've got two good ones."

With that she bent her pale arms toward me, hands palm up as she stood to face me.

"See?" she said, with a look of pride.

I automatically winced as I saw the raised, ragged lines of

pink skin commemorating her failed attempt at finding her own way out of a life she felt was simply too painful to continue living.

"Well," she continued, "where are they, your scars I mean?"

"They're in a place people can't see them."

Her eyes suddenly got soft and empty, almost trance-like. An eerie, almost wicked smile seemed to rise up from someplace deep and dark within her, a kind of primordial response triggered by the mention of a private place in me.

I felt suddenly cold and ill. It was as though I were staring into a maelstrom and if I didn't break the gaze we shared I might become trapped in her nightmare. She swayed toward me, her flimsy dress catching a bit of the breeze from my open window.

"I know all about them secret places; I know what men want, what they need from women."

She was just a foot away from me now and continuing to hold my attention with an almost hypnotic stare. Her deep blue eyes were magnetic, attempting to pull me toward her and down into her abyss.

The cold within me changed suddenly and something warm and wonderful took its place. I flashed back to my own childhood and the night my cat was struck by a car not twelve feet from my front door. I had rushed up and gathered him in my arms, whisked him inside, placing him in a shoe box. I remembered him looking into my eyes, hurting and helpless, the death gurgling in his throat, his breathing rapid and shallow—in, out, in, out—then nothing. That same compassion was here now, in me, with us.

She arched one eyebrow as she very slowly and deliberately reached up with her right hand, her scarred wrist turning away from my gaze. He fingers played with the shoulder sleeve of her dress, deftly sliding it down, exposing a freckled shoulder. I knew I must be as tender and thoughtful now as I had been with my cat those many long years ago. I slowly and carefully extended my left arm toward her and slid the sleeve back up and in place.

With that she came to and her mouth opened to speak but no words came forth. Her brows furrowed as she squinted and slowly shook her head in incredulity.

"I don't want anything from you, Gloria, except, maybe to be your friend, if you'll have me."

Suddenly she appeared shocked, as though she'd been struck in the face. She began to shake and quake like a rag doll or marionette. Years and years of pain and loss began rocking her physical frame and her emotional anguish came rushing up and out of her in great racking sobs from someplace deep within her devastated spirit.

Instinctively I reached for her, careful to encircle her in my arms, yet keeping a necessary distance between our two bodies. Her face found my chest and her forehead began to gently beat against it. Her grief stained my shirt with ancient tears. A million years and a greater number of ruined lives sped by as if powered by some invisible yet knowing and caring heart. Finally, the still following the storm arrived and we stood together, this little girl-woman and I, tasting a healing moment of grace.

Slowly, deliberately, she looked up, her tear-stained hair obscuring one blue eye. Her mouth was open slightly as if she were about to say something, anything to rescue us from this terrifying moment of self-disclosure. I placed my hands on her shoulders and gently kissed her forehead. She pursed her lips shut and sobbed quietly for a moment. I heard a bird whistling somewhere in the distance as if calling on his friends and neighbors to witness this newly-formed friendship between a broken man and a wounded child. We sat side by side on the bed just then, looking out the window on this strange yet wonderful town, just a few hours' drive from the City of Angels.

CHAPTER NINE

Morning came as it always did: unannounced and uneventful. Days are like empty parkas, just waiting to see what we'll fill them with. Where did we get the idea that someone else will do the honors for us? I had come to the conclusion long ago that that was the problem with too many folks—me included—that we whistled while fate wilted only to find out much too late that "the fault lay with us, Dear Brutus, not in the stars, that we remain such underlings," with much apology to Shakespeare or whoever actually penned those sentiments.

Still in my underwear, I rubbed the sleep from my eyes and took a seat at the desk. The town was awake now and the folks who called it home sweet home were all busy doing their or someone else's thing.

I noticed a woman in her thirties in the distance looking in a store window with a teenage boy by her side whom I assumed was her son.

Instantly I was back in my hometown again. High school days. Something about that woman's hair style—soft, reddish brown, shoulder length curls—brought me back in memory to another woman I'd shared a bus ride with almost daily. I've had some strange experiences with women, believe me, but some stand out in bold relief more than others. This was one of them. After all these years, I still have trouble believing it took place at all.

Nearly every morning as I boarded the bus and took my seat on one with its back to the side, I would invariably see her leaning against the window in one of the two passenger seats perpendicular to mine. Within minutes, she would look directly into my eyes. I knew it was inappropriate, rude or some such, but I simply couldn't or wouldn't break our visual connection.

And neither would she.

For almost half an hour we would sit and stare lovingly into each other's eyes. I suppose one of us should have found it embarrassing but if we did, we didn't care enough to alter our gaze. I thought she was breathtakingly beautiful. I remembered wondering if she were a motion picture star; but how could that be in the Midwest?

And then came the fateful wintry morning when she got off

downtown at my stop. She had never done that previously. I remembered because after I was off the bus and on my way up fifth avenue toward the stop where I made the connection to go to my high school I would often watch her as the bus left. She would still be looking out the window at me, smiling, as if she were my mother (she was old enough to be certainly) wishing me a good day at school.

But not this day. I stumbled down the cold, slippery metal stairs and turned slightly only to see her right behind me. In all those mornings we had never exchanged even a word. Not one syllable. Yet we had communicated flawlessly nonetheless. Her eyes had always seemed like liquid pools of loving affirmation. For the life of me I could never fathom what our silent sympathy for each other was all about. But it was beautifully real and nurturing. And here she was now standing in the snow and slush right beside me as the bus pulled away leaving a trail of diesel fumes and the sound of ancient brakes releasing and gears reluctantly meshing. Her smile broadened and she opened her lovely mouth.

"Are you catching another bus?"

"Yeah, I transfer about a block or two up Fifth Avenue."

"That's where I'm going, to my store. May I walk with you?"

As I nodded she lifted her right arm up toward me and I quickly encircled it with my left. She leaned closer to me. I wondered how we might appear to onlookers, this thirty-something woman and a young high school boy still very much awash in male hormones. I don't remember ever feeling so proud to have someone on my arm, not at the sophomore semi-formal, nor at the junior prom. This was different, real, adult, like in the movies. I wanted the walk to last forever and didn't say a word when we passed my bus stop. She looked up at me, eyes twinkling, bundled up in that warm, brown overcoat with the fur collar, looking for all the world like Vivien Leigh in an old Alfred Hitchcock picture.

"Are you sure you don't mind walking with me? The store's just up ahead."

"Nah, really, it's my pleasure."

It had never occurred to me that there was no reason at all for my doing this. I suddenly got a cold chill and not from the winter weather. It had never dawned on me that this wonderful woman might be, and probably was, married!

We were in front of the store now. I slid my arm out of its embrace of hers as she pushed the glass door open. She turned, smiling broadly. "Come in; just for a minute. I'd like you to meet my husband."

I nodded sheepishly and followed her inside the very high-end merchandise store. My family had certainly never ventured inside an establishment like this. In front of me stood a good-looking man in his mid-forties with a strong jaw, curly, close-cropped salt and pepper hair and a broad and engaging smile.

As if on cue she said, "This is...."

"...Chip," I offered.

"Chip," she continued. "We ride the bus together nearly every morning. He was nice enough to walk me up here on his way to his bus stop."

He nodded and smiled even wider. "Well, what a nice fellow. You must come in some time and try on some clothes. I'll be sure and give you a discount for being so kind to my wife."

I blubbered something or other as I shook hands with him and backed away toward the door.

"Well, I better get to work" she said with a happy tone in her voice. I could imagine her singing.

"Yeah, and I better get my bus," I replied.

"Thanks again for keeping me company; I get a little afraid sometimes walking downtown alone. It was nice having a strong young fellow like you with me on such a cold morning."

"I'll be seeing you" I mumbled as I quickly left the store and strode deliberately back toward the bus stop I'd intentionally passed earlier. I felt as though I were walking on air and decided that she was the kind of girl I'd marry all right. Someone loving and nurturing and sweet and pure.

I was sitting on the bus now, looking out the grimy window,

forehead pressed against the cold glass, when I realized I didn't even know her name.

CHAPTER TEN

I was standing on the porch of the diner, hands on my hips, debating whether I ought to venture on over to my good buddy Jim's automotive emporium when I felt something push the back of my knee. I spun around to see the "Beav" looking up at me, television squint firmly in place, baseball cap tipped back on his curly black hair.

"Almost tripped ya up, didn't I?" he chuckled.

"You did."

"How's about you and me toss a few?"

I crouched down and looked into his freckled face.

"Shouldn't you be in school?"

"Nah; it's Saturday. There ain't no school today."

"Isn't; isn't any school."

"That's what I just said. You makin' fun o' me?"

I pulled his hat down over his eyes and he began to fake yell, "Hey, this guy's tryin' ta work me over! Help!"

"Go on in and ask your mom if I can take you out to the park in the square for a few minutes."

His eyes widened in disbelief and he whirled away, slamming the door behind him. I didn't even have time to reconsider my stop at the mechanic's before the little guy had rejoined me, tugging at my right hand, pulling me off the stoop and onto the street.

It was a lazy morning and only the occasional local was making an appearance either at the post office or millinery or drug store. The entire area really did remind me of the "back lot" at Universal. Yet is was real, or unreal, depending upon your perspective. I had nearly given up on trying to figure the place out. But I realized it couldn't be done anyway, at least not by yours truly.

Everything was greening up about now. It seemed as if no one was particularly interested in what a middle-aged guy and a young boy had in mind for a Saturday afternoon. Sammy was way ahead of me now, running into the middle of the park and taking what he thought was the position of advantage for our little game of makeshift sport. A few mothers were scattered around the well-kept lawn and some preschoolers were working out on the swings and monkey bars. The little guy seemed completely oblivious to them. He was intent only on impressing me with his pitching skills. I couldn't help liking the little twerp. Despite whatever had gone on between him and Gloria, he had apparently escaped relatively unscathed, and that without any significant father figure either. I had to admire the kid's moxey. He was made of tough stuff all right. I only hoped it would stand him in good stead as he navigated his way through what could only be termed a more difficult life than he deserved.

"Go easy on me, okay? I'm an old duffer."

He tossed one in my direction and I grasped it easily whirling my arm around and throwing it back a little off of direct center so he would have to work a little to snatch it up. He grabbed it and shot it back to me with a smile on his mug like he'd swallowed the sun.

"Where did you get those muscles?" I asked as I caught his pitch.

Smiling broadly he fired the ball back to me, just over my head, causing me to really stretch to keep my catching record intact.

"Must be all those pancakes your mom shoves your way."

"Must be." He winked as he wound up and let fly. The ball stung my palm this time.

"What're you tryin' to do, murder me?"

He burst out laughing as he caught my pitch. Then he just stood there, hands on his hips, eyes squinting in the sunlight.

"You got any kids?"

"Why, you looking for a dad?"

"Maybe; you interested?"

"Seems like something your mom should have a say in, wouldn't you say?"

He walked over to me and socked me softly in the breadbasket. I put my arm around his head, pulling it against my abdomen.

"You got some muscles too," he said in a muffled tone.

I scratched his back and then we separated and made our way over to a vacant picnic bench where we sat down as I took a candy bar from my jacket pocket.

"Hungry?"

"You betcha," he said as he whisked it from my hand.

"You're a smart little fella, you know that?"

He shrugged his shoulders.

"I guess so," he replied as he eyed the gooey mess he was working on.

"I'll just bet your smart enough to take care of yourself; know what I mean?"

He nodded. "Yeah, you mean about not talking to strangers and, like that."

"Like that," I said.

"Your body belongs to one person: you. You know that, right?"

Suddenly, his eyes got misty and he looked off into the distance as though he were waiting for someone to write his response on the clouds so he could just read them to me verbatim. Then he looked down. After a long pause he looked up at me again.

"People should leave a guy alone if he don't wanna be bothered."

"They should indeed," I agreed.

"'Specially when they're bigger'n you are and lots heavier and it ain't even real wrestling or anything 'cause when they pin the guy on TV they lay over him sideways....*sideways.*"

"You got that right," I concurred.

"I reckon it's a guy's right to give 'em the boot and not play a stupid game like that anyway."

With that he lowered his head. I reached over and tussled his hair. He took a big gulp of air and then sighed it all out.

"That pitchin' kinda made me tired, but a good kinda tired; know what I mean?"

"C'mon, let's go see what your mom's doing about now."

He took off at a run, a slightly embarrassed but greatly relieved little man.

CHAPTER ELEVEN

When I got back inside I went up to my room, showered, shaved, dressed and sat down at the desk. I pulled some writing paper out of the rickety drawer and began making some notes on the events of my stay so far. I hadn't been writing long when there was a knock on my door. Audrey poked her head in.

"Chip, I wanted to thank you for what you did with Sammy today. It's like he's a different little guy or something. Just what exactly did happen anyway?"

I turned and smiled at her.

"Ever work out with a punching bag?"

She shook her head.

"Well, let's put it like this. You can work out more than a sweat with one."

Her eyebrows crinkled.

"Your little boy had a few good rights and lefts in him and I didn't punch back."

"I don't get it," she replied.

"You don't have to. Now, how would you like to go on a real, live, honest-to-goodness date tonight? You know, in that other town."

She pulled back, answering as she closed the door. "You don't have to ask me twice. Gloria can watch Sammy and I close early tonight anyway. It's definitely a date!"

I nodded, smiled and turned back to my notes. I expected to have a few more pages to add before this was all over.

Taken all together, the interpersonal stuff hadn't done anything but help me and hopefully Audrey and her kids. But the car deal, the phone situation and the feeling of being followed, the mysterious car I thought I saw following me in Belleville, not to mention gunshots, those were things a bit more dangerous and potentially significant. No matter how I re-set the pieces they didn't fit. As the saying goes, *"You're not paranoid if they really are out to get you."*

But who?

Rick seemed stupid, ignorant and annoying, but a gun?

The Creep at the service station was probably too interested in kiddie porn or some other perversion to get physical with a total stranger.

Audrey certainly didn't have any motive and besides, she was with me when that shot rang out in the park.

No, it didn't make any sense.

There was the red paint on Rick's bumper, but, giving him the benefit of the doubt, I hadn't really looked very closely to see if it was an exact match to mine. That line of thinking led me straight back to a cast of characters from my past.

But what past?

I really couldn't think of anything or anyone I'd done that would provoke stalking, scaring or silencing me permanently. I certainly wasn't a threat to any other screenwriters. My stuff usually went straight to video and Hal handled all of the financial end of things. I was usually paid WGA scale or a bit more and sometimes got a point on the "back end" of a picture, assuming it got made, which mine usually did. But a disgruntled producer, actor, writer, or even a crew member? It just didn't add up. More and more I felt I should just dump the puzzle pieces back in the box of my somewhat scrambled brain and rejoin the "madding crowd" in LA.

But what about Audrey?

The sun was just setting when I followed her downstairs and we left the restaurant together. I opened the passenger side door for her, bowing as I did. Chip Delaney: date par excellence. She snickered and slid in. I hadn't experienced the tingling I was enjoying as I opened my door since the night of my sophomore semi-formal. My friend and I were able to borrow his brother's red GTO. Those were the days. My dream date and I had the time of our teenage lives all right. Even though thirty some years had come and gone I could still remember the climax of that evening. The music stopped and we continued dancing. Something out of an early *John Hughes* movie. God rest him.

"So where're we goin'?" she asked as she tilted her head a little, looking at me with narrow eyes.

"You sure do like that perfume don't you?"

Smiling broadly, looking directly in front of her she replied, "If it ain't broke, don't fix it."

"You got that right. The first girl I ever smelled *Rive Gauche* on was a waitress at a restaurant I worked at one summer. I was a first class bus boy and developed first class heat resistant hands to go with, that year. Anyway, I got one whiff of that stuff as I filled those empty plastic bays with dirty dishes that I followed her all over the place all night long."

"Did it go anywhere?"

"Nah, she was a couple years older than me at the time, when the age difference mattered."

"I'm familiar with it," she said.

"I'll just bet you are."

She leaned back against the seat cushion and traveled back in her memory, a wistful smile making its way to the surface of her beautiful face.

"What?"

"Oh, I was just thinking of a young kid I met years ago when I was modeling."

"Really? Do tell." She sat up in her seat again.

"I was doing some *Sears & Roebuck* stuff at the time I think...in a local mall. Anyway, after the evening's fashion show this lanky high school age kid came around the entrance of the dressing room. I was probably about twenty or so at the time. So I asked him what he wanted and he hemmed and hawed his way into asking for a date."

"No kidding? How'd that work out for him?"

"It was kind of a poignant moment actually. I very slowly, very deliberately, very delicately, declined. By that time I'd already been 'round the mulberry bush' too many times to count. I really didn't want to poison him with my contagious, questionable morality. He seemed way too innocent."

"And?"

"He kind of sighed his nerves out in something akin to relief."

"I don't understand."

"I think maybe he'd seen me on the runway that night, and somehow figured dating me would affirm his masculinity or something. He didn't look like a football player if you get my drift. Deep down I'm sure he realized going out with me wasn't really going to change him. I was a million miles away from his concocted, preconceived projection of me. He smiled weakly and left, relieved. I never saw him again."

"Wonder where he is now?" I asked.

She sniffed and smiled and looked up at me with mischief in her eyes.

"Craziest thing you ever did, you know, on a date or something remotely similar?"

I eased back in my seat as the lights of oncoming cars winked at me on their way by.

"Got to be that goofy summer when I was about sixteen or so."

"And...?" she queried, looking up at me a little sideways, a squint forming on her freckled eyelids.

I smiled at her and presently put my eyes back on the road and my mind decades in the past where I found myself on the back porch of one of my friend's houses.

"She, my friend's mom, used to hang her wash out on the line in the backyard."

"You're joking!" Audrey added.

"I'm not; so, there, that definitely dates me, eh?"

"Definitely," she responded, nodding at the dark highway

stretching out in front of us.

"Anyway, this guy's mom was really quite something. She was just finishing up with the clothesline deal when I walked into the backyard looking for my friend."

"Where's this going?" Audrey asked.

"In retrospect, nowhere good," I responded.

"Anyway, I offered to carry a couple of baskets of clothes inside, to the cellar. I remember it was just starting to drop dark. It was the end of summer; I can even remember the smell of the screen door as we entered through the basement. She was beautiful to my high school eyes. Very thin, very fit and pert with short, blonde hair and pale blue eyes. She always wore bright red lipstick."

"That's quite a memory."

"She was quite a mom."

"And...?"

I nudged the wheel a bit to correct an unconscious weave I'd drifted into.

"She was a widow, you know; a war widow. She was making her way up the basement stairs as I was bending over to set the baskets down. I guess I kind of lost my balance straightening up and sort of slipped and fell onto the stairs. If I try, I can still smell that blue paint. She turned quickly, alarmed, and came back down, sat right next to me on the step."

"'Chip, are you all right?' she asked, sitting there next to me."

"'Sure,' I responded. And then it seemed like time sort of stood still and I got kind of woozy."

Audrey looked over at me, a serious searching behind her beautiful eyes.

"The next thing I knew, she touched my cheek with her hand. Without thinking I put mine on top of hers. She leaned toward me and put her other hand around my neck. I was kissing her before I knew it and she was kissing me back as I encircled her back with my arms. I don't think we were there for more than fifteen minutes or so but it was one of the most unusual, erotic and at the same time, loving experiences I'd ever had. I almost imagined myself in uniform, returned from Vietnam, returned to Carol."

Audrey laid her head back against the seat cushion again, closed her eyes.

"What?"

She smiled, eyes still closed.

"Don't break my heart, Chip."

It was dark when we pulled into the restaurant parking lot. There was a light directly overhead that made the buckle on Audrey's high heel sparkle as she got out of the car. I put my arm around her and she slid hers around my waist. The lot was almost full and I was wondering if we would have much of a wait as I opened the door. Before I could even get my bearings, a young twenty-something brunette, menus under her freckled arm, asked "Two?" Audrey nodded and we followed the girl into a dark back room of the place. Music from the seventy's added all the ambiance we were going to get and we slid into the mock leather booth in the corner. A tolerable rumble of conversations surrounded us like cotton candy and the greeter placed the menus in front of us.

"Ricardo will be with you in a minute." She smiled. "Can I get the two of you some waters?"

Audrey nodded and smiled in the affirmative for the both of us. I leaned forward, my arms on the table, fingers interlaced.

"What?"

"Nothing," I replied. "I'm just wondering how I got lucky enough to have my car assaulted in your hometown."

She laughed and glanced around the place before responding. Her eyes seemed to glaze over as they settled on me; she leaned forward, too.

"Maybe you sinned in a previous life."

"I wouldn't be surprised. If you're my punishment, 'let the games begin!'"

She rested her chin on her hands.

"Chip, what are we?"

I scanned the room before answering. Then I allowed my

eyes to settle on her oval face.

"Good question. One I've been considering since I arrived in town. We don't fit in any category I'm acquainted with. But I'm open to establishing a new one."

Her response was interrupted by my cell phone signaling a text. Odd, because I wasn't expecting any communication of any kind from anyone.

"'Scuse me just a tic," I said as I looked and opened the message.

"Tonight is the last night of your lives."

The words stood out in bold relief. Ordinarily I would have blown it off as just another bit of annoying but harmless spam. No way to trace the origin, either. *"Unknown sender"* put the kabosh on any further inquiry, at least from me. To say I'm technically-challenged would be the understatement of the century.

"What is it?"

"Hmm? Oh, it's nothing. Another unwelcome cyber solicitor's all."

She nodded, convinced, just as the waiter appeared. He was a tall fellow, with earrings in both ears. I'd been told one on the left meant "straight" and one on the right meant "gay." Apparently, the jury was still out with this guy.

We ordered but my appetite had fled the premises. The rest of the meal and evening went by in a nervous blur. If Audrey noticed my preoccupation, she didn't let on. I was glad. Having to explain yet another unexplainable phenomenon would have really overtaxed my already overwrought nervous system. Whatever had been happening for the past week or so seemed to be headed inexorably to its predestined climax if you believe in kismet, destiny or some such. I didn't really have much left in the area of beliefs. I did, however, have a sense that something was about to give and it didn't bode well for either of us. I couldn't think of anything else to do but play it out and see just where this night took us. I glanced at my strap watch and it read nine-thirty. We'd be back in town around eleven o'clock or so and, much as I'd planned to be earlier in the evening, I wasn't in the mood for *amore.*

The diner and gas pumps were dark with only a few security lamps on ancient poles illuminating a now starless night. Audrey looked down at her pumps as we made our way into the building. She fished her keys from her purse, turned the handle and I followed her in. It was dead quiet. Gloria had been in charge of little Sammy and they appeared to be safely asleep upstairs. It was then that I noticed a dim light under the door of the storage room across from the restaurant's dining area. No one should have been in there at this hour and I highly doubted Sammy or Gloria had been or were there now. I put my index finger to my lips and Audrey nodded in understanding as she followed me over to the door.

It was as I turned the knob that both of our "lights" went out.

Funny how some things in life seem to go full circle. It had only been a century or so since I'd been knocked unconscious for the first time in this little town. I could only suppose this was one for the road. Wearily and warily I raised my head, one eye open, the other cemented shut by dried tears. I pried the lid apart and my eyes slowly adjusted to the semi-darkness. No use struggling, there was only enough duct tape securing my arms and legs to the chair to hold *Secretaria*t for an hour or so after the bell. Audrey—still unconscious—was similarly secured. I heard a cough from out of the shadows. Then a deep breath, then another wheeze. It was familiar all right. I'd heard it on and off for days now. The voice that followed started out with a creak like a front porch rocker from prohibition days on a plantation in Georgia.

"Have a nice meal?" he peeped.

"Go to hell."

"You first, my boy; you first."

Audrey stirred. "Chip, Chip, where are we?"

I answered her without taking my eyes off the patch of darkness from where the aged voice originated.

"Still in the storage room: against our wills, I might add."

"Evenin' lady," he interrupted.

"Who are you?" she asked between hacking coughs.

"I'm an old friend of Chip here, from way, way back. He ever tell you he was a professor?"

"What's this about?" I demanded, trying to rock myself free from the constraints.

"It's about ruinin' a young person's life and karma kinda catchin' up with ya and bitin' ya on the bee-hind: *hard*."

"How did you get in here; are the kids okay?" Audrey demanded.

"Never mind 'bout them children, darlin'; they're jest fine and dandy. Though I can't promise I'll be able to say the same for yous two in jest a bit."

My eyebrows scrunched together in concentration as I tried to place that voice. It was in my cranial hard drive somewhere but I couldn't access the information; apparently I lacked the appropriate application.

"Got a special thing fer kids as a matter of fact," he continued. "Why, it seems to me that a feller what ruins a young person oughta be taken to task. Take that there mechanic, fer instance."

"You know Jim?" Audrey queried.

"Jim, jam, whatever; it don't matter now."

"What are you talking about?" I interjected.

The voice chuckled and cackled before spilling the contents of its owner's twisted mind.

"I stopped by the shop on the way here to meet you. It was completely empty, bein' after hours an' all. Anyhoo, I heered this radio a-playin' old-time rock 'n roll and sees this lanky fella leanin' over his desk a lookin' at some photos. I gits up kinda close and looks over his shoulder, real quiet an' cat-like."

"What do you s'ppose he's a-lookin' at?"

Audrey shook her head slowly.

"Yer little girl, that's what. And in what they call a 'compromisin' position, too, with a two-bit, one-eyed mechanic more 'n five times her age."

"Gloria," I sighed in sadness.

"The very one," the voice added.

"So I jest stepped back inta the darkness and waited. Sure enough, he stuffed the photo back in the drawer and got back under that there Wrangler he'd a-been a-workin' on."

It sickened me to think of that slimy snake of an excuse for a man ruining a young life like Gloria's. I tried to console myself with the thought that our brief interaction had possibly begun her emotional mending. Audrey was crying now and moaning "Gloria" softly to herself.

"But he got his, he did," the voice added in somber finality.

"Ever see what happens when a car jack slips out from under whiles a feller's still underneath a-workin'?"

We just sat there, staring into the darkness.

"Well, it kindly sounds like a great, big watermellon's a-breakin', kindly slow-like. Then they's a squishy kinda thumpin' sound like when little ones is a-jumpin' on an old mattress. Only with some real serious yellin' a-goin on at the same time."

He snickered and laughed.

"That ol' boy screamed like a woman. But he died like a baby, cryin' for his momma."

I swallowed the bile that was forcing its way up my throat. Audrey's head was down on her chest now, moving to and fro as though she were trying to rock the madness away.

"What does all this have to do with us?" I asked again.

"Nothin' in particular, that part don't."

"Then what?"

"I'm more concerned with another young lady, a bit older, when you got your hands on her, and ruined her life. Imagine a college professor-type what breaks a young coed's heart and gits her knocked up to boot. What ya figger that kinda feller deserves, eh?"

"Marilyn was my granddaughter and you oughta have known better; 'specially with yer background."

"Marilyn?! The girl from college? But I...we...were never intimate, I swear!"

"You swear? Shove it. They's only been one Virgin Birth,

brother and it weren't Marilyn's.

Audrey stirred and stared at me.

"Chip, what's he talking about?"

"He's talking about the girl I mentioned to you, the one I got too involved with, the one that ended my teaching career due to the scandal."

"But you said...."

"I know I did and I meant it; this guy's got this all wrong."

"I'll tell you what he deserves," he continued. "He deserves to be stalked and scared and beat about the head with his car smashed up and his girlfriend threatened with gunfire...and then killed damn dead along with her, that's what."

"Audrey's got nothing to do with this; she's innocent."

"They's no such thing as innocent. We come inta this earth wrong and that's jest the way we live and die. Some worse than others along the way. I'll be damned if I don't make things right for Marilyn."

His last phrase acted like a doorbell ringing and bringing recognition at last to my benumbed brain. "*I'll be damned*" echoed in my head like the cleats on my high school shoes on an empty hallway floor.

"By the way," he cackled, "thanks again fer the tip 'bout drainin' me 'radiator;' bendin' these ol' knees works like a charm, really starts the flow all right. Just like you recommended."

"So he'd followed me all along, beginning with my last trip to Hal's office," I mused to myself.

No wonder he was always one step ahead. My car being smashed, the phone calls, the gun shots, the car appearing to be tailing me, even the text on my cellphone: all designed by my self-appointed judge, jury and now, executioner; and all for a crime I hadn't committed.

He stepped out of the shadows, the lone, dim, overhead light causing the halo of gray on his bald head to sparkle in the dark. He was holding the most powerful handgun I'd ever seen. It was a *Taurus* model they'd nicknamed *The Judge*, just like the one I'd described in my most recent action script. Only this one wasn't loaded with blank cartridges and it was aimed directly at us.

"Chip...," Audrey tried.

"Here's what I'm-a gonna do," he continued.

"I'm gonna slip around behind yous two an' cut yins loose. Then I want yous ta get up, real nice and easy-like and stand over there by the door inta the dining room o' this here dive. And no funny stuff 'cause this ain't no laughin' matter and I ain't a-waitin' fer another opportunity. I reckon I'm pretty well satisfied with the pain I put in yer noggins. It ain't gonna bring back that little girl I raised, but it'll hep me sleep a bit better at night knowin' I sent your woman to hell, with you a-followin' close behind her."

"What do you mean, 'bring her back'?" I asked as he cut the tape while holding that cannon with the other.

"She off'd herself, is what I mean. Canceled her own ticket and with a gift ta write like she had. Kin you believe it, 'professor'?"

I stood up slowly, my legs almost completely numb from being immobilized for God only knows how long. I watched, helplessly, as he undid Audrey's restraints. She stood slowly, wobbling, as she moved toward me as he had motioned her to do. Her eyes clearly revealed the hopeless sadness of the situation we were in. We stood there, side by side, holding hands like school children, being taught our last life-lesson by a lunatic who had been pushed over the edge by what he perceived to be the ruination of his beloved granddaughter.

"I didn't do it...with Marilyn."

"Save it," he snapped. "You was all she ever talked about; she fell fer ya, *hard*. And now you're a-gonna fall, an' yer 'little girl' here is gonna watch. I'm not a-gonna finish ya easy-like, either. No, I'm a-gonna jest loosen yer knee cap first. Then I'll put one in blondie's chest an' you kin watch her bleed out. See how you like watchin' yer loved one suffer. Then, I'll put one right between yer lyin' eyes."

I heard the snick of the hammer just as Audrey's elbow stabbed me in the chest as she leaped in front of me. There was a flash and a crash as the explosion rocked the room and the spent shell shoved the two of us against the wall with the force of a jackhammer. I cradled her in my arms as we slid to the floor, the smell of cordite filling the room. I was looking at his grimy boots as Audrey's head lolled to one side against my chest. She was cooing softly, "Jesus loves me this I know...for the Bible tells me so...little ones to Him belong...."

Then she coughed and hiccupped and breathed out her lost life.

I looked down at the ever-widening crimson stain in my chest, watched the rich, red blood leaving my pain-wracked body. We must have looked like quite a pair lying there, dying, alone in that darkened storage room.

My heart was breaking for poor Audrey: unlucky at life and unlucky at love, dying in the arms of someone like me. A hack writer...a "burned out" college professor...and fallen-away priest.

BLACK SUNRISE

The sky looked like the back of a broad's black chiffon blouse.

You know the kind: with spider-like fingers of thicker thread fanning up and out from the solid cloth below the shoulder blades. And the sun struggling to elbow its way through the strands of pollution and failing, providing an eerie contrast between what should be and what stubbornly is.

I found myself at the bottom of a ravine as near as I could figure. My horse was long gone and I can't say I blamed him for "gettin' outta Dodge." I would have gladly gone with, if I hadn't been tossed, ass over teacups, when he spooked and reared at the backfire and blast of exhaust when they made it away from us.

* * * * * * *

I guess it all began back at the *Bottoms Up Bar* where I was cooling my jets and looking over the facts on the case they'd dumped on me. There seemed to be fewer and fewer rangers available lately and more and more cases, and I know my way around a horse and...well you get the idea.

Kramer slid this one by me before I could decline so there I was nursing a beer and reading all about Joe Jiminy (I kid you not) and his alleged involvement in a "B & E" that left a rich old duffer of a family practitioner with a squashed skull, an empty safe and a missing wife.

More like a daughter.

Don't you get tired of clichés?

Of course life is where they come from, isn't it?

I remember a writing class I took back in college. I wrote up a little mob piece and described the protagonist as a rough-hewed feller with a long scar from eyebrow to chin on his left cheek.

The teacher really took me to task over that one: called it "clichéd" and "devicey" and informed me that no editor would ever take it seriously.

Like he would have believed me even if I'd told him I was describing a distant relative!

Anyway, I decided to go on out to the doc's place and examine the crime scene for myself.

The house and surroundings looked about how you would expect them to. The building itself was an overdone brick, stone and wooden affair with one of those wrap around porches you sometimes see in Queensland, Australia today, or the American south of yesteryear.

I tethered Bill (my trusty Quarter horse) to the porch rail, dismounted and saw nothing of interest either in the yard nor nearby. The house itself was set off from the main road and even that isolated thoroughfare was fairly quiet with only a few luxury cars parked nearby and what looked like a lawn care company van situated near the corner.

I slowly made my way onto the front porch and peered through the slits in the blinds on the small window in the front door. I tried the knob and it opened unexpectedly. The cool blast of the air conditioning unit greeted my perspiring body and I was mighty glad of it. The ride over there, though not much over two hours on horseback, had been under the hottest sunlight of the day. Even though it was getting on towards sunset, the damage had already been done as far as my aging anatomy was concerned. I was happy for the overhang of the porch roof shading my old pony outside.

Now I don't consider myself overly brainy or anything but

anytime there are a couple of decades or more difference in spouses' ages and the "Mr." is rich and the "Mrs." isn't, my gut starts to tingle just a little bit.

Everything looked jake and I was prepared to agree with the crime boys when I heard a tinkling sound coming from the rear of the house. I wouldn't say the window exploded or anything, but it definitely resisted an unwanted advance.

I'm a big fella an' all, but I don't like being cold-cocked any more than the next guy so I slipped my Colt .38 detective special from its holster and backed against the wall. The sun was just beginning to say goodbye for the night and deep shadows filled the room, darkening the design on the oriental carpet where I stood, rock still and waiting.

The tinkling was replaced by giggling.

Then the most beautiful twenty-something blonde my blood-shot orbs had ever had the pleasure of eye-balling came in, accompanied by the usual accomplice. One of those tattooed idiots with the perpetual "What's it to you?" look on his pock-marked face. And the blond crew cut with yet another tattoo visible in the center of his pointy dome. The lingering light caught the top of his head as he bent over, revealing the words, "What, Me Worry?" etched in deep, red ink.

I took a deep breath and let it seep out, nice and easy like. I figured it'd be a lot simpler to just reconnoiter rather than to tip my hand this early in the game. At this juncture, I didn't even know the rules.

While I was musing along this line, the two of them were slowly and quietly going over the place in a desperate search for something of apparently great value, at least to the girl. They were moving in and out of rooms, up and down the hallways of the doctor's digs, checking corners and crevices, openings and other things that might serve as signposts toward their recovering the missing item(s).

I was alone again: with my thoughts and my gun and my breathing.

Or at least I thought I was.

Very faintly I heard what sounded like panting or gurgling or gagging.

I was just beginning to wonder if maybe the good doctor had left a servant of some kind behind: against their will. I heard the rear door open and close and I breathed easier, figuring young "Bonnie and Clyde" had left the building, presumably searching yet somewhere else for Elvis or whomever had gone missing.

The vocal sounds were replaced by a scratching noise. Slowly and carefully I stepped out and followed the sound to a cupboard deep in the back of the well-appointed room. With gun in hand, I moved to the side of the door and slowly turned the polished brass knob with my right hand, pulling the door toward me.

The panting began again and I stepped around placing me eyeball to eyeball with him.

"Maybe they're shooting the next installment of *Men in Black*," I said to myself as the little fawn-colored Pug stared up into my blue eyes with his wall-eyed brown ones. He looked like he was smiling, mouth agape and panting.

"What's your story?" I asked.

Right on cue, his mouth closed, the panting stopped and the smile was replaced by a look of deadly seriousness as he cocked his head to one side with an expression that looked for all the world like pity for me.

I crouched down and his smile returned as I scratched him behind the ears. They felt smooth like velvet. His eyes were shiny, globular marbles and nature had worked the fur on his forehead into a well-defined fleur-de-lis. My guess was, this was the little dude for which Blondie had been searching so diligently. At any rate, he was safe now.

I moved to the kitchen, filled his dish with water and set it down near the doorway. Right on cue he trotted toward it, his sharp nails making a ticking sound on the ornate marble floor. He was drinking like there was no tomorrow, his little belly moving up and down rhythmically. Then he finally stopped, stepped back, licked his lips and looked up at me with an idiotic smile just before he suddenly spread out on the cool tile, his front paws on either side of his chin which was flat on the floor, making him appear like a little canine sniper. His large kind eyes followed me as I looked around the kitchen in search of clues. It occurred to me that he looked as if someone had somehow fit a human being into a dog's body.

"Note to self: purchase a Pug at earliest convenience."

I was starting to wonder exactly what was what when I heard another sound, this one definitely human...and female, if I could trust my forty plus years of meandering around the fair sex. The Pug continued to follow me with his eyes which were slowly closing from boredom. Me? I could use about a lifetime of it. But that was a luxury I couldn't afford right now. I had a murder/robbery to solve. Or at the very least, to gather a couple of clues concerning.

I realized the sound was definitely coming from upstairs: the far bedroom I would guess.

So how in the world did a dog and an unknown female elude the searching gaze of the CSU?

Who would return to the scene of a crime to deposit one human and one canine?

And where did the young couple fit in?

While I was musing along these lines the sound became a voice, a rather nice one if I may say: insistent and pleading for assistance from the first unlucky ranger to enter the domicile. I grudgingly obliged and began my ascent of the stairs, the sound of my boots apparently disturbing a canine dream of some kind as the little guy's paws twitched. His squashed face resembled a baby's as it passes gas. Maybe he was dreaming of finding just the right tree to mark for posterity.

I was in the corridor now, the voice calling out "Help" with the regularity of a metronome. It was coming from the back bedroom all right and I wasn't taking any chances. I had my .38 at the ready when I opened the door of the overly done master bedroom of the "silenced sawbones." It was a rather gaudy affair with a lot of shine to it from silken sheets to silver shavers on the nightstand. I moved toward the walk-in closet and announced myself.

"Deputy Ranger Shelton, here," I barked in the best professional voice I could muster. "Are you all right?"

"Yes...but please...get me out of here!"

With that I slowly unlocked the door and was greeted by the "original" of the young blonde I'd seen previously prowling the first floor.

"Well?" she intoned, rather indignantly.

"Well, well," I returned and grunted my way onto my knees to undo her restraints.

"Thank you," she said, sardonically, shaking her freckled arms free and getting herself up onto her sandaled feet. I raised myself up in concert with her.

"Did you get him?"

"Did I get whom?"

Exasperated by my apparent stupidity, she repeated the question.

"I said, did you *get* him?"

I folded my arms over my chest.

"Ma'am, I'm not sure to whom you refer."

She clicked her tongue and walked to the window, the faint moonlight making her appear almost angelic. She was quite something all right. As if reading my thoughts, she looked over at me as though she were examining an extra-terrestrial. I was beginning to wonder myself if I hadn't dropped down from outer space, what with the alien looking dog and all downstairs.

"Why don't you sit down and we'll have a chat," I offered as I took a seat on the plush red chair in front of the vanity.

She clicked her tongue again and sat on the edge of the bed, opposite me.

"Name, rank and serial number." The ice began to thaw and she smiled at that one.

"I'm Kay Hawkins, the doctor's wife, of course."

"Of course," I nodded.

"Aren't you going to ask me if I'm all right or something?" she asked.

"No need for that, that I can see," I returned.

She simply pursed her beautiful lips.

"So here we are then," I added.

She squinted at me. "Here we are."

It turned out that she'd heard the sneak-thief enter the house but was sucker-punched from behind before she could even press any alarm buttons (and the house had plenty of them). She had been unconscious during the entire episode, only stirring when the young couple's breaking and entering routine had roused her from her unwanted sleep.

"What about the CSU?" I asked.

"CS what?" she countered.

"The crime scene unit that investigated this business."

"Well, if there was one, I wasn't aware of it. I heard and saw nothing: nothing at all."

That explained an awful lot. So there was no investigation prior to mine after all. Why would Kramer send me up here to follow up when there had been no preliminary? And how did he know Jiminy figured into this? And just exactly how was that couple of Pug-chasers involved? My head was beginning to hurt trying to fit pieces of a puzzle together that seemed to come from different boxes.

"Mrs. Hawkins, as I said, I'm Ranger Shelton and I was sent up here to follow up on...to...ah, investigate...."

"Yes...to investigate the robbery?"

"I'm afraid it's a bit more than that," I offered.

"You see, your husband...your husband is deceased."

Her face nearly exploded as she gasped, "What?!"

I reached over and patted her tan forearm.

"Just calm down, Ma'am. We're going to take this very slowly."

With that, the emotion drained out of her face and she sighed into herself as she seemed to fold inward, any remaining emotional strength slowly oozing out of her body as her shoulders slumped in defeat, her expression empty and nonplussed. She looked up, asked weakly, "Dead, really dead?"

"That's what my supervisor said, yes."

She shook her lovely head from side to side as though she were being hypnotized.

"I just can't believe he's gone, dead: murdered."

I pursed my lips trying to think of a rejoinder to that one.

"Can you think of anyone who might want to harm your husband?"

Looking vacantly at the floor she responded woodenly. "Not a soul. He was very well liked, Vernon was. Working here was almost like being a country doctor for him, only with a much wealthier class of patients of course."

"No doubt."

She looked up at me with those unusual blue eyes, almost cobalt-colored, but with tiny flecks of lighter blue floating in the irises. "Robbery I can understand, but not murder, definitely not murder."

I sighed out some exasperation and folded my arms over what used to be a six-pack that might have passed with a significant push years ago.

"Anyone else live here, on the premises?"

She pulled a face and looked away from me at that one.

"April...my daughter...doesn't live here exactly, but does show up often and at rather inopportune times, usually looking for money."

"She the one the pooch belongs to?"

Touching my forearm, she gasped, "My God, don't tell me Barney's been hurt."

"No," I reassured her.

"He's downstairs sleeping off a belly full of water."

She smiled brightly. "Thank God he's all right; he's like a little deformed son to us."

"Kinda grows on you I would imagine."

I was just going to suggest to her that she take a trip downtown with me to make an official statement, when the telephone rang. She looked at it, startled, then at me. I nodded and she answered it.

"Yes?"

She shrugged her shoulders at me.

"Why I wouldn't have any idea; I certainly didn't. No, I don't know when another time would be convenient." She hung up the phone.

Her eyebrows bunched together.

"That was a lawn care service."

"One you normally use?"

She squinted, as though trying to make some sense of the call. "No; that's the odd thing. He sounded like I knew all about the appointment."

"And when was that?"

She shrugged. "He said this afternoon, at four."

Suddenly, she looked up at me with the expression of a child asking permission of a teacher to use the restroom.

"I'm thirsty suddenly. Would you mind terribly if we continued this downstairs?"

"Not a bit," I lied. I was actually thinking of a nice, cold beer someplace back in town. "I wouldn't mind whetting my whistle either."

She smiled stiffly and I followed her downstairs and watched and waited at the table while she fixed us up with two iced teas. Pug opened one sleepy eye only slightly and went back to canine dreamland where he could chase another school bus. What would he do if he were ever able to catch up with one?

She evidently noticed my admiration for the little nasally challenged half-pint.

"As I said, his name's Barney. Been with us for about six years. You'll notice the black on his muzzle is starting to turn gray. It happens earlier than folks think. They actually used makeup on 'Frank' when they did the second 'Men in Black' picture."

"Guess he did need 'dental' after all then, didn't he?"

"I imagine."

She suddenly just stopped talking and looked at me with those very unusual eyes. I was so intrigued I could only return her stare. She tried to say something, paused, changed her mind and then resumed her gaze. I was beginning to sense a familiar stirring in the usual places. This was starting to become "awkward," as they say in merry old England.

She sighed.

"I can't believe he's gone; the doctor is dead."

I leaned back in the chair.

"Mrs. Hawkins...."

"Kay," she interrupted.

"'Kay,' I don't think there's too much more that can be done about things right now. You're absolutely certain you didn't hear anything downstairs earlier, before the break-in, nothing at all from the crime unit search?"

She shook her head in a deliberate "No."

I looked through the kitchen window into the star-filled night on display. Presently I returned my gaze to those mesmerizing eyes of hers.

"What does your gut tell you?"

She looked down at her shoes, the wheels turning within her beautiful blonde head. Her eyes returned to mine again and a smile began to slowly creep onto her pink cheeks.

"Maybe I can help a bit."

I whirled around to identify the source of the voice but before I could draw my weapon I heard the snick of the hammer on his.

She nodded approvingly and rose from her chair.

"It's about time; I was beginning to wonder if you'd received a better offer."

He smiled wickedly.

"Darlin', there ain't a better offer than yours on this side of the universe. Just had a coupla things to take care of is all."

"And what are we supposed to do with him?" she asked.

He sniffed in disgust. Then he put his hands on his hips as he inwardly deliberated the dilemma of them being saddled with a Texas ranger who had just now outgrown his usefulness. He smiled in triumph.

"I think we just take him a ways out of town. Maybe he and

ol' 'Trigger' had a little riding mishap on their way over here, you know, to check things out."

"Why there was a robbery and a murder, wasn't there?" she said, poker-faced.

He smiled broadly at her.

"That's right."

It looked as though someone had somehow turned up the power behind those strangely entrancing eyes of hers. They appeared luminous now as though they had been transported from another world altogether.

"You can get up now, officer," he intoned somberly.

"That's 'ranger,' if you don't mind."

I stood.

"I do mind and I don't give a rip about what you call yourself."

Disgustedly she added, "He's a small cog in a large wheel is all."

He motioned me toward the front door and I reluctantly did as I was told by the wave of the small canon he held in his right hand.

It was cool and dark now as I mounted my horse and he tethered my hands to the saddle horn. The moonlight caught her eyes as she looked up at me with an odd expression of delight.

"You just follow my car and he'll follow you; very simple, even for a 'country bumpkin.' Simply, 'follow the leader;' understand?"

"Perfectly," I rumbled.

A couple of last minute adjustments by them sent us on our way.

During the ride I allowed myself to drift off into "alpha-ville," that in-between state where the brain is in daydream mode and the body relaxes. My horse and I had navigated all kinds of terrain in all types of weather under sunlight and moonlight. He was practically "bomb-proof." I say "practically," because he did spook and land me in that ravine right on cue as they'd planned when they left us miles away from nowhere in particular.

Oh, and did I mention that I was blindfolded during the entire episode?

My guess is we were at least five miles from where we'd started out and I had no idea which direction from the house that was. I do know it had been all back roads and rocky paths and a patch of woods where lonely owls serenaded our little impromptu caravan.

I heard the brakes on her car complain a little and I relaxed in the saddle, pulling up slightly on the reins and bringing my horse to a gentler stop than either vehicle's. The doors opened and slammed in unison and I listened to their footsteps make their way over to me.

There were four pairs of them.

"Who've we been joined by?"

He chuckled. "Hey, hey the gang's all here!"

"Great, let's have a party," I grunted.

"'Fraid the party's over, at least as far as you're concerned," she announced.

"Now why doesn't that surprise me?" I offered.

I heard the scuffle of feet, listened to them discussing their final preparations.

"April, you and Jason take Barney with you across the border and just check into the hotel and wait. For God's sake don't give the dog any Mexican food."

"We know better than that, Mom."

"We got it all under control, Mrs. Hawkins. We did the house bit okay, didn't we?"

"I want to believe that, Jason. Just don't disappoint me."

My friend with the gun added his two cents worth.

"An actual 'double indemnity' clause. James M. Cain would be so proud of this deal."

She responded with a breathy, "Close to five million dollars."

"Plus the contents of the safe," he added.

"Which will unfortunately never be recovered," she said.

"Unfortunately," he agreed with a chuckle.

I could sense the seriousness of his next question.

"How much did Captain Kramer get us for, for getting this joker involved?"

"Only fifty grand," she said.

"What a piker!" he added with a click of his tongue.

"To the hungry soul, every bitter thing is sweet," she concluded.

"He's pinning it on this low-life Jiminy character?"

"That will be his story, yes," she replied calmly.

My head was spinning.

The facts of this case were whirling around my fuzzy brain like swaths of cotton candy, surrounding my slowed thinking like so much invisible gauze.

There was absolutely nothing I could do about any of this, now or later. It was all sewn up tighter than the handkerchief around my head.

The stranger concluded his end of the conversation with, "I guess I can finally say goodbye to this lawn care van and all that goes with." With that, they kissed. I heard her moan, him groan and her daughter's car engine suddenly roar to life, spraying gravel toward me and my horse.

As Bill reared and I left the saddle, Kay's lover's last remark replayed itself in my mind as I prepared for a painful landing on the rough and unforgiving terrain below.

I mused, "So, the gardener did it."

MOONLIGHT AND ROSES

On the morning of January 18, 1995 the last thing I expected to do was die.

Don't get me wrong; it had been a mixed up affair from the beginning. But I must have looked a little like a character from a Raymond Chandler novel, standing there under the streetlight, the damp mist giving everything a strange halo. I looked down at the ever-widening crimson blotch on my shirt, winced in pain and pulled my trench coat together around my sore middle. I was dying all right...but I'm getting ahead of myself.

It started out as the best weekend of my life. I was in Santa Monica to sign off on a deal on my first screenplay sale. It had been quite a ride. Exactly how does a horse trainer from a small Mid-western town break into the movie business? I couldn't speak for anyone else, but I didn't quit my day job, that's for sure. I'd gone through a rather painful and messy divorce a few years back, and thankfully, the muse had arrived before I'd become a serious drinker. I wrote myself out of a blue funk with a novella that came, either from my childhood, or Jung's "collective unconscious."

Not long after that I was watching a martial arts picture when I realized the star would be perfect for the lead role in my book. I got his agent's address from the Screen Actor's Guild, wrote him a complimentary letter, enclosed a copy of my book and fired it off to tinsel-town. I actually cried a few months later when I received a hand-signed letter from him. He loved the book and thought it would make a great film; oh, yeah, and "why didn't I adapt it into screenplay format and send it to his agent?"

I did and his agent took me on, on a "piece by piece" basis. In other words, I was free to submit scripts to him anytime. If he liked my work, he'd send it out. If he thought it was crap...well, you get the idea.

Then a week ago, the call came. Could I come out and sign off on a "small" $12,000 script sale—direct to video—which I'd written for another action star my agent represents. I could, and I did. Sure, it was less than half of the "Writers' Guild Minimum," but it would take a lot of horse training to gather that much money in the amount of time I'd spent on that screenplay (about 40 hours, total). And what did I care if they had someone rewrite me? This wasn't Macbeth; more like McDonalds.

I decided to spend a few days of vacation time and took a room at the Loew's. I'd had lunch with the actor who'd bought my script and he turned out to be a really nice guy in person. Amazingly, he only wanted a couple of changes, and he wanted me to be the writer to make them.

I'd read somewhere that the odds of an "unknown writer" selling a screenplay are about the same as winning the lottery. Yet I'd done it. "Hooray for Hollywood!"

I was so wound up after lunch and my meeting with the action star that I needed to relax. I went back up to my room, drew a bath and was just about to ease myself into that warm, bubbly water when I heard the commotion next door. I slipped into my jeans and pulled a tee shirt on, walking softly to the door of the adjoining room. It sounded like a man and woman arguing and escalating into a physical confrontation. Instinctively, I knocked. "Hey, is everything all right in there?" I asked. The noise dropped off and I heard someone "shooshing" someone. I stepped back from the door and waited. Nothing. I shrugged my shoulders; mission accomplished. Then there was a knock at my front door. I opened it and the woman who stood in the doorway shocked me. I could feel the pulse in my neck; she was that gorgeous.

"Excuse me," she smiled. "I'm sorry if we disturbed you. But it's only the middle of the afternoon and, well, Jack—my friend, and I—were just going over some lines for a play we're both auditioning for. We both work here in the hotel and the management lets us use empty rooms for practice."

"Not a problem," I lied. "I just thought there might be something wrong."

She smiled again, slight dimples decorating her pale cheeks. "It's a love story; you know, 'true love gone wrong'," she said, rolling her eyes.

I nodded and slowly moved back from the doorway. "Good luck with your audition," I added.

"Thanks," she smiled as I closed the door. "Maybe there's a script here somewhere," I thought as I got into the tub.

I didn't think about the incident again until the following evening—Saturday—after another dreary, overcast day. I went to the Broadway Bar & Grille in Westwood. I was making notes on some script changes while drinking my beer and working on a too-large burger. I looked up and recognized the girl, presumably with "Jack," at the bar; and still *practicing*. He'd gotten so loud the other customers were getting uncomfortable. This wasn't a dive and I seriously doubted this place was allowing them audition rehearsals too. To my and the other patrons' astonishment, she "paint-brushed" him, right there at the bar. The slap sounded like a small firecracker. With that, she swiveled out of her seat and made for the door. He snickered, rubbed his cheek, shrugged his shoulders and turned around to finish his drink.

As I watched him in the mirror, he looked vaguely familiar to me. "Maybe I've seen him in a commercial," I thought, and went back to my notes. But there was nothing doing. All I could see was that beautiful, gutsy actress. I decided to follow her. I left enough cash on the table to cover my check and a generous tip. For once in a long time, I was flush. I'd taken my agent's advice and cashed the check at his bank. "You never know about deals," he'd told me.

I watched her from a bit of a distance and then followed her for a while before stopping at the Santa Monica Pier. It was closed and I didn't think it had done much business anyway. Maybe all the rain had dampened everyone else's spirits, too (no pun intended).

"Hey," I called. "Don't I know you?"

She whirled around and smiled in recognition. "What are you doing out in this drizzle?"

"Looking for love in all the wrong places," I replied.

She stopped and leaned her elbows against the cold, green, metal railing. She looked down at her white, high heels and then up into my eyes. "Maybe not," she said, seriously. "Go for a walk?" she asked, looking for all the world like a lost, little girl. I extended my arm and she wrapped hers up in it. We headed down the pier, along Ocean Boulevard. She spoke of her hopes and dreams, leveled with me about her rocky relationship with Jack, the alcoholic wannabe, soap opera star. We stopped at several places for numerous nightcaps into the wee hours of the morning. I admitted to following her from the restaurant and she thanked me for caring enough to do it.

Eventually, we wound up back at the pier and I was actually beginning to wonder if I ought to stay in LA a little while.

That's when I heard the footsteps behind me.

She moved away; I turned and then felt the reality of what I'd only written about previously. The blade in his hand felt like a hot wire searching my stomach for my spine. All I could do was gasp.

She smiled as she went through my sport-coat pockets and retrieved my wallet: my fat screenwriter's wallet. Her smile widened as she looked into Jack's eyes. His were looking into mine and then I remembered where I'd seen him.

It was at the bank, yesterday morning, when I was cashing my check.

STALKING SUSAN STORM

Action star, Susan Storm, huddled in a dark bedroom closet. She held her breath as she deftly slipped her cell phone from her belt. The bedroom door creaked open, heavy footsteps slid across the carpet. She whispered into the phone, "Travis, if you're there, don't pick up. I think he's here, in the house, in my room. He thinks I'm alone. I can't call the police; they're in on it. Travis, honey, you're my only hope. Just get over here as fast as you can!"

Suddenly, the door swung open, Susan screamed and the director shouted "Cut!" She sighed, smiled and slumped against the door jamb as the film crew began to take down the equipment for the scene. The director grabbed her by both arms, peered intently into her eyes, and affirmed, "That was great! This one's gonna put you right back on top and then some."

She smiled, poking his chest with her finger. "Let's hear that again on opening night." He nodded, patted her on the back and grabbed the clipboard from an assistant.

* * * * * * *

Screenwriter Tom Paige filled out the last line on the express mail sheet, slid it across the counter to the clerk and tapped the package. "If this thing sells, I'll buy you a hamburger."

"Yeah? Whatcha got in here anyway?" the middle-aged man asked. His balding head was beaded with perspiration and his expression one of the "seen it all" variety.

"Hopefully the next big hit for Susan Storm."

The clerk shook his head. "Movie people," he lamented to himself as he turned and tossed the package in the appropriate bin behind him.

* * * * * * *

Susan whisked into the dojo, bowed at her sensei and the other class members and then slung her duffel bag over a chair. She slipped out of her shoes, bowed again and took her place in the class. Her instructor paired her off with Stacy, a pretty but masculine-looking student in her early thirties. They exchanged smiles and began working on techniques. Presently, Stacy threw Susan and then assumed the "mount" position, attempting a one-arm front choke-hold. Susan countered by rolling her opponent's right arm over into a "chicken wing," assuming the dominant position, her face close to Stacy's ear. Stacy whispered over her shoulder, "I could get to like this." Susan eased off the pressure, furrowed her eyebrows at the "pass" and slipped off, springing up onto her feet.

Later, after class, in the dressing room, Stacy smiled and invited her to share a bite of supper with her at a small Chinese restaurant close by.

"Actually, I have plans, with Joe; he's my steady guy right now," Susan offered. Displeasure spread across Stacy's face.

"Oh, I didn't know. I'd heard about your divorce and figured...."

"Yeah," Susan smiled. "But that's behind me now."

Hopeful, Stacy added, "If you change your mind...."

Susan pursed her lips and countered with, "Thanks; I'll keep that in mind."

Stacy touched Susan's arm gently. "Sometimes it takes a while before you really figure out what you want."

Susan smiled artificially and slipped by her and out the door into the evening.

It was shortly after this that Joe and Susan shared a bite of supper at a small table on the pier at Santa Monica. The setting sun's rays caught the blue of her eyes while gulls flapped overhead and a cool breeze blew in off the ocean.

"What's up with you tonight? You seem bothered." His pale eyes narrowed in concentration.

She jabbed at her salad with her fork. "I was just wondering why I can't be 'anonymous.'"

"You? Exactly how do you plan to pull that one off?"

She looked off into the distance, her eyes clouded over with thoughts of fans intruding into every aspect of her life. She stared into his eyes.

"I mean it. First the very nasty divorce and the deadbeat still won't stay out of my life. Now, even the dojo isn't any relief. A fellow student hit on me today!"

He chuckled in response. "So, what do I have to do, buy you a couple of full-length mirrors? God, Susan, you're young, beautiful, famous—we won't even mention your figure—what do you expect guys to do?"

Clearly exasperated, she added, "This time it was a girl!"

He winced, shook his head and laughed.

"Seriously, Joe, she really seemed angry when I passed. Makes you wonder about somebody doing something, I don't know, crazy."

He sucked a tooth and patted her arm. Flexing his muscle, he offered, "Look, feel my muscle; I'll protect you."

"Oh, you," she laughed. Then her smiled faded into an expression of concern.

* * * * * * *

Hands smoothed a clipping from one of the "trades," affixing it to the dank, dark basement wall which was nearly covered with photos and stories featuring Susan Storm. This one's headline read, "Action Diva's Divorce Turns Nasty." A voice whispered, "Your 'ex' hasn't really experienced 'nasty.'"

* * * * * * *

Susan's agent, Hal Mitchum, sat across the desk from executive producer, Arnold Zahn. The pudgy, balding "suit" "steepled," his fingers on his desk blotter, leaning his bulk closer to Hal.

"Look, Susan's a little 'soft' right now. Who's gonna keep buyin' her bustin' guys up? She's got a killer body, you know that; have her do this one for us, will ya?"

Hal squirmed, pulled a face. "Look, Arnie, she's just not going to do 'adult stuff.' She's got a little girl now; forget about it." Zahn frowned, leaning back in his chair.

"I got pressure on me, fella, from—shall we say—interested investors; understand?"

"No, I don't," Hal countered. "Susan's movies always make money; they're pre-sold internationally even before the cameras roll. What's the problem?"

"The 'problem' is they want her to go in a different direction. You gotta convince her this 'new' angle is the best angle, for her, for everybody."

The troubled agent pressed, "And if I don't?"

"You don't wanna go there; believe me, Hal, you do not wanna even go there." Hal sighed in defeat.

* * * * * * *

Stacy made her way from the dojo to her car in the dim glow of the street lights near the parking lot. Suddenly someone grabbed her from behind. Strong hands grasped her throat.

"Wait," she grunted, "I'll give you my purse, money, whatever." The choke-hold only tightened.

"I don't want your money and Susan don't want your attentions, get it?" The forearms cinched tighter.

She nodded quickly. "Susan, okay, yeah, all right."

* * * * * * *

Susan opened her front door, threw her purse on the hallway table and headed straight for the kitchen. After nearly emptying a bottled water from the fridge in one go, she hollered for her daughter. "Tiff, any calls?"

The precocious twelve year old scampered to the top of the stairs and shouted, "Just dad and he says he wants to talk to you right away." Susan frowned. "Okay." She dialed his number and began a guarded conversation.

"What? You wonder why I did *what*?"

Stan, her ex-husband, sighed, rolled his eyes.

"You mean to tell me Joe or one of your martial arts buddies didn't bash in all four windows of my Land Rover?"

Exasperated, she sighed out her response. "Absolutely not. Why would any friend of mine do anything like that to you?"

"Why wouldn't they?" he countered. "It's a shorter list. And by the way, what's the idea of giving your 'beaus' the specifics of our settlement? There was a note pinned to my car's only unbroken piece of glass that read, 'pay up or be shut up: *permanently.*'"

"What? Stan, I have no idea what you're talking about. Just file a report with the police. I'm sorry about your car, honestly; and I haven't told anyone anything about anything relating to us." Unconvinced, he sighed in disgust.

"Well then someone who reads the trades must have friends 'in the know.'"

"I'm sorry," she replied weakly.

"Yeah."

She hung up. Tiffany shouted from upstairs. "Mom, can we have Pizza Hut tonight?"

Absentmindedly Susan answered, "Pizza Hut, whatever, honey."

* * * * * * *

Tom Paige sauntered into his kitchen, poured himself a glass of water from the tap and quickly dropped it into the sink as he noticed what looked for all the world like a masked person staring at him through his kitchen window. In a moment, his front door splintered open and the person sprang in and behind him choking him with one arm and "chicken-winging" Paige with the other. The startled writer winced in pain.

"Look, we can work this out; seriously, I'm not rich, I'm just a screenwriter for God's sake, the bottom of the food chain, but I'll give you what money I have."

His uninvited visitor grunted into his ear, "Money? You hack! Your money's not worth the paper it's printed on to me. It's dirty; dirty money is all you have."

"Hey, I may be a lot of things but I'm not a thief; what I write *I* write. What's this about anyway?"

The individual loosened the grip, spun Paige around and tossed him into a living room chair. "Don't get up, you creep." The screenwriter put his hands up in mock surrender as the stalker took a seat opposite him.

"How could you do it? How could you write that pornographic trash for her? You really think she'd dirty herself playing that part, you louse?"

Taken aback, Paige responded, "My script, my action script for Susan, *that's* what this is about? Look, it's a job; I write what I'm hired to. What's this got to do with you? It's her decision."

"*Her* decision? I don't think so. Who hired you to write that piece of crap for her? Who did that?"

"Zahn, Arnie Zahn; he and his backers. Don't quote me on this but I get the feeling he's 'connected.' But what's the difference? I don't even know if she's read the script. I sent it to her directly; I'm sure her agent will have something to say about it, too."

"Mitchum? He's a mug. He doesn't have any business getting her involved in the sordid trash you write. He should be taking better care of her."

Paige massaged his sore neck. "Is that so? And I suppose you'll make sure that happens?"

The masked intruder sniffed in disgust. "You can count on

that." Then he rose up, towering over Paige who attempted to scrunch lower into the chair.

"I don't think you'd handle your computer too well with broken fingers. Most people don't know that it takes over a year to fully recover from a broken finger: over a year."

Paige moved his hands behind his back, sitting on them.

"You never write anything for Susan Storm again. If you get offered a contract on this one, you refuse to sell; you absolutely refuse."

Paige nodded quickly, perspiration dripping from his forehead.

"Hack!" And with that, the stalker stormed out of the house.

* * * * * * *

Susan's agent, Hal Mitchum, called his cat while setting a dish of food on the kitchen floor. The silence puzzled him into a slow search of the downstairs where he discovered the cat—dead—on the bathroom sink counter, a pink ribbon tied a note to the small animal's neck. Shocked and stunned, he slowly unraveled the paper which read, "Susan Storm does the 'Paige' script and the next ribbon circles *your* neck."

He stumbled back and out of the room, flopping into a high-backed recliner. He fumbled the receiver off of its cradle and punched a number. Producer Arnold Zahn answered on the first ring.

"I thought you said you were being pressured to *have* Sue make that soft porn script. So why am I being threatened to have her *not* do it?" He scanned the room with nervous eyes. "*You* have no idea? *I* have a dead cat; yeah, a dead cat and a death threat. You tell *me* who."

* * * * * * *

A young Susan Storm swung back and forth on the rickety swing set in the schoolyard playground next to her best friend.

"So, who're you gonna marry anyway?" Joanie asked.

A group of young boys were fighting over a dropped ball within earshot of the girls. Susan slowed her swing to a stop and Joanie's kept pace. Susan interlocked her fingers and twisted her arms "inside out" in embarrassment. She quickly looked back and forth, moved closer to Joanie and whispered, "Laawee (Larry)!"

Joanie at first appeared disappointed. Then they both burst into loud giggles. Young Larry dropped the ball he'd just captured and stared at the girls, mouth agape.

* * * * * * *

The firm hands pasted yet another article on the basement wall, and the voice whispered, "But 'Laawee' isn't married, yet!" Then standing, hands on hips, squinting eyes scanned the headline: "Clouds Rising Over Storm's Career?"

"Susan, how long do I wait? You promised. What more do I have to do? I watch you, protect you, follow you, love you, but all from a distance; a safe but sad distance. What do I have to do? When you were that little girl you...."

The dark eyes widened within the mask as "the penny dropped."

* * * * * * *

Susan and Tiffany were sparring in their basement gym. From "fighting position" Tiffany rushed her and knocked her mother off of her feet. Susan slipped the protective gear from her daughter's head and tussled her hair.

"Hey, what's the big idea?!"

Tiffany laughed and repositioned herself, firmly straddling her mother's waist.

"So, do I get to try some lipstick for Melanie's party tonight or not?" she asked, eyes narrow, head tilted. Susan sighed.

"If I don't agree and quickly, I'll never have time to get

ready to meet Joe. Okay, okay; but just a little. Don't mask your natural beauty."

"Oh, Mom," she mugged.

Susan continued. "And be careful walking over there."

Tiffany attempted to reassure her. "It's only a couple of blocks and besides, I'll have my cell phone and my special bracelet."

Susan nodded. "I know, I know, the one with the little penknife on it. And speaking of cell phones, leave yours on the 'vibrate' setting. If you can't *hear* it over that stuff you call music, at least you'll *feel* it! I still want you to be extra careful."

Tiffany rolled her eyes and back-flipped off of Susan. The action star watched her little charge scramble upstairs, shaking her head with love and admiration.

* * * * * * *

Joe and Susan were leaning on the cool green railing as they looked out over the city from the observatory atop the downtown skyscraper. Various other couples whispered hopes and dreams to each other in the roof top's other corners. Traffic lights twinkled below as he gently touched her arm, turning her toward him.

"I guess this is as good a time as any."

"For what?" she asked, smoothing her hair back.

He sighed, turned away, speaking to her as he looked off into the moonlit night.

"You know I fell in love with you the first day I saw you."

She nudged his arm, "Joe...."

He slid her hand off, looking away again.

"No; let me finish. I've been needing to say this for fifteen years." She turned her back to the rail, folded her arms in front of her and cocked her head, her eyes watching him intently.

"Go on then."

"When you came into that journalism class, late, arms full of books like a little school girl, when you scanned the room and then planted yourself next to me, I thought my heart would stop.

You were absolutely the most perfect woman I had ever seen in my life."

Her eyes narrowed, completely taken aback by the information.

Joe continued. "College was a living hell. If someone even said your name or if I saw you from a distance my pulse would pound so loud and hard I was sure I was having a stroke!" He pursed his lips, sighed and slowly turned to face her.

"Sue, I guess what I'm trying to say is, while I'm not happy about your divorce, I'm not going to cry about it either. We never really connected in school—Stan made that impossible— but what about now? Is there a chance for us now?"

Her eyes misted over as she looked up and into his. She took his face in her hands. "My love," she whispered. And they kissed.

* * * * * * *

An unwanted stranger watched from behind a tree at a distance as Tiffany closed and locked the front door behind her. In the blink of an eye she was whisked from the street and into the waiting vehicle.

* * * * * * *

Susan and Joe enjoyed a lingering goodnight kiss in front of her house. He skipped down the steps and jogged the block to his parked car. Before he could even use the keyless entry he was jumped from behind. A vigorous fight ensued with the stranger getting the better of Joe, despite both of them utilizing martial arts skills. Joe, dazed, looked up from the pavement into the masked face of the person towering over him.

"What's this about...who *are* you...why...?" he mumbled. "Why?"

Joe's assailant looked back and forth at the empty intersection and then turned and faced the injured man on the ground.

"Because there is no way on earth I'm waiting for another marriage to start and fail. Uh,uh; no sir, no even way. She's mine. She's gonna marry *me*. She promised and she's gonna keep that promise, even if it means I gotta do somethin' to that little rugrat o' hers."

Joe whispered groggily, "Tiffany."

* * * * * * *

The film crew busied themselves with the set-up of the next scene while the director huddled with Susan in a corner of the set.

"You okay?" he asked.

"Oh, I dunno; Tiff slept over at a friend's last night and didn't leave me my 'good morning mom' message. She knew I had a six a.m. call. She would have left it last night."

He smiled and waved her off.

"That all? Sue, she's becoming a little woman now, you know. Maybe you're going to have to make a little room for one or two young men. You were breaking hearts already at her age, weren't you?"

She nodded in agreement, smiling weakly. "Yeah, I guess you're right. Let's get this shot done so I can check my messages again, okay?"

Waving his hand in defeat he sighed, "You're hopeless!"

* * * * * * *

Tiffany scanned the basement walls, eyes wide with terror, as she viewed the story of her mother's life paraded in front of her. Photos, stories, magazine covers and articles papered every available inch of space. She jiggled her rope-tied wrists yet again, the penknife pendant getting closer to her being able to open and use it.

* * * * * * *

Susan burst into the hospital room, sat on the bed next to a battered and bruised Joe Churchman.

"You look like you've been 'rode hard and hung up wet'; for God's sake, what happened?"

"I feel like I've been *kicked* by a horse!" he whispered. "I don't have any idea who it was; but whoever it was, wore a mask. And it was definitely about you."

"Me?"

"You. What can I say, you've got some kind of 'guardian angel,' only a 'dark' one.'"

"I came as soon as I got your message," she added.

She smoothed his hair back. "Joe, I'll come back again a little later, but I really want to stop home. I still haven't heard from Tiffany. It's got me bothered, and now with this...."

Looking almost guilty, he added, "I didn't want to mention this on the phone, but Tiff was mentioned; Sue it sounded like some kind of back-handed threat." She sprang up to leave.

"That's it; I'm going home to check on Tiffany." He nodded.

Outside Joe's room she stopped, back to the wall, took a deep breath and began to shake and cry softly. She tried to pull herself together as she made her way down the crowded hall, but the sign for the hospital chapel arrested her attention. Hesitantly, she entered the small empty room. The candlelight gave the chapel a soft glow and a crucified Christ seemed to look down on her as she took her place in the pew. She leaned back, closed her eyes, breathed in the sweet smell of incense and sighed out some of the tension of the past few days. She looked up at the statue, whispered her thoughts.

"It's been a long time. I'm not sure I know how to do this. It's just that I've tried to be so strong for so long and I'm just not. And I don't want to be, not anymore."

She lay her forehead on the backs of her hands resting on the pew rail. Again she looked up, stared at the small altar where candles mutely symbolized prayers ascending. She began to sing softly, weakly. "Jesus loves me, this I know, for the Bible tells me so. Little ones to Him belong...." She began to shudder as her tears came stronger.

"Tiffany...."

She wiped her nose with a tissue, looked up at the porcelain statue.

"They are weak, but He is strong."

Presently, a door opened and a nun entered, saw Susan weeping and walked over to her, putting her arm around her shoulder.

* * * * * * *

Susan entered her house with quiet determination. She took a deep breath and punched the play button on her answering machine. "Thursday, three p.m. 'Hello Susan; oh, and Tiffany says hello too. She had such a nice time, no, not at her friend's, but with *me*. I think we're going to have to have a change of plans. You see, it's not going to work out with us after all. So I'm thinking I'll just adopt little Tiffany here and wait until she's a "big girl." Then I can marry *her*. Maybe she's not a liar, like her mother.'"

Susan shook her head in disbelief and confusion, surrendering herself to the chair next to the machine.

"'And don't even think about contacting the police, not if you want to see Tiffany again. I've gotta figure out what I'm gonna do with you. And I do have a lot of options. You see I know everything about you. Everything.'"

A series of images swirled within the twisted mind of her stalker, scenes: outside Joe's hospital room, at the far corner of the rooftop where Susan and Joe spoke, outside of Zahn's office while he met with Hal Mitchum, and as a fellow student at Susan's dojo.

"'I even know where you live.'"

The final image was that of the postal clerk's hands as they hefted Tom Paige's screenplay package, the government employee's finger moving back and forth under Susan Storm's home address. He remembered smiling as he sniffed in satisfaction while he watched the screenwriter leave the post office that afternoon.

"'I just may show up there when you least expect it. I may make Tiffany an orphan. I may be on my way over to your house right now, while you're listening to this. Maybe I'm already *in* your house. I'm just not sure what I'm gonna do and you can't be either. I'm gonna like it that way: liar!'" The machine beeped. "End of messages."

Susan's eyes carefully scanned the downstairs of her home. Slowly, purposefully, stealthily, she began a thorough search of each room including every closet and other possible hiding place. She continued the same process upstairs, finally making her way into her bedroom. Closing the door behind her she was nearly at the head of her bed by the window when she heard heavy footsteps on the first floor. She slipped into her bedroom closet, closing the door in front of her. She held her breath as she deftly slipped her cell phone from her belt. She slid her thumb over the numbers.

* * * * * * *

Tiffany cut her wrists loose from the ropes. Her cell phone vibrated. She lifted it to her ear, heard the familiar voice.

"Tiffany, it's mom. Don't answer me. If there's any way you can get away, do it. He may be in our house right now."

* * * * * * *

Susan punched the off button of her cell phone. She waited inside her bedroom closet, breathing heavily, waiting patiently, to surprise her assailant. Slowly, she lowered herself into a sitting position and closed her eyes. The sound of floorboards creaking startled her. "Your car's here; that means *you're* here. C'mon Susan, let's talk, for old time's sake. Tell me again how you're gonna marry 'Laawee.'" She squinted, then her eyes widened in disbelief at the recollection of a childhood statement all but forgotten. Savagely, he yanked the closet door open. She screamed as they began a long and involved physical confrontation testing the martial arts skills of both of them. Battling from room to room, the stalker finally seemed to have the better of her, choking her against the hallway wall.

Suddenly, the sound of Tiffany's scream filled the hallway as the young girl sprinted toward them and rushed in, catching him behind the knees. He tumbled backwards over her, landing flat on his back. Tiffany followed her move with a vicious elbow strike to his throat which caused him to pass out. A relieved Susan scooped her daughter up into her arms, looked through tear-filled eyes into Tiffany's. They hugged and sobbed in relief; the stalker lay unconscious behind them.

* * * * * * *

Susan and Tiffany sat beside Joe's hospital bed. He smiled with relief at Susan. "Hello, Love."

She returned his smile. He reached for Tiffany.

"Hello, Pumpkin." She hugged him and he settled back on the pillow.

"God, I'm glad you two are safe. I felt so helpless here."

Reassuringly, he added, "He's going away for a long time where he won't be stalking anyone or anything. Still, I promised to be 'strong' for you. I guess I didn't do too well in that department, did I?" He sighed in disappointment.

Susan looked at Tiffany, then at the crucifix hanging on the wall. "That's okay. I think I've found another source of strength."

He squinted, puzzled by the comment and then the three of them shared a hug.

WASHROOM TALK

Clinking, clanking and clattering.

The room was buzzing with sights and sounds of conversation and infatuation. This was the place to reconcile, reconnoiter and reconsider. Guys and gals jostled and jousted. The ladies were in waiting, while the gentlemen were painting, scenes of serious situations aimed at more than momentary sensual delights.

The room was stuffy; the air was being drained from it by an invisible, airborne vacuum cleaner. Smells and scents meshed and clashed and drifted upward toward the clear, summer night. It was more than a restaurant or bar. It was an oasis, a mirage really, offering temporary respite from the corporate climb. Collins was a rest stop on the highway of the "here and now" existence of twenty-first-century urban achievement. It was a breath-catcher, a nerve-saver, a stitch-in-time to save nine-to-five yuppies from becoming permanently set in stereotype.

Gloria's conversation was passing straight through Paul's head, unnoticed. He scanned the crowd wondering why he was here and just exactly how he could escape from the incessant guilt and shame that surrounded him like some ancient shroud placed upon his shoulders by an undisciplined and over active conscience.

"Where are you?" she asked.

Startled from his reverie, he responded. "Here's the waiter now."

A tall, thin, and tan cologne-sprayed individual arrived with the menus and began describing the various specials and drink deals. Gloria's voice was so many gnats, persistent and annoying. Somehow, Paul managed to place their orders while she chatted on, endlessly, about everything and nothing.

He became aware of a pressure that seemed to start at his arches and push its way up into his middle, perhaps looking for an escape through one of his heart valves. He needed to leave the table, *now*.

"Paul, where *are* you?" Gloria asked again. Her exasperation was growing, adding to his inner turmoil.

Evasively, he added, "I'm just at sixes and sevens on several deals all at once, Glor. Maybe if I just slip out to the men's room I can wash up a bit and clear my head a little."

Unconvinced there wasn't something a little more sinister below the surface—like his dumping her for another woman— she acquiesced with a weak smile.

"I'll just be a tic," he reassured her.

With that he was up and off to the rest room, leaving her alone in the crowded restaurant with her thoughts and fears and insecurities, now made worse by his admitting being preoccupied. Unfortunately for her, she seriously doubted his guardedness had anything remotely to do with corporate shenanigans of any imaginable type or variety. She was sure there was a dark horizon in front of them, all right. Gloria put her chin in her hand in defeat, her elbow resting on the table, her parents' childhood cautions against the practice notwithstanding.

* * * * * * *

It was cool in the men's room. The lone window was opened about two inches allowing the soft breeze from the gathering night to enter unhindered. The slight smell of a lemony cleaner of some kind caused the tiny hairs on his neck and forearms to tingle. It enabled his psyche to travel hundreds of miles and dozens of years to the high school he'd attended. He remembered the sanctuary the boy's room had been to him "long ago and far away." Remembered how he'd almost hid there for as long as possible before going back out onto the baseball field only to be forced to endure yet another round of the jeers and sneers of those in his class who weren't as "athletically-challenged" as he had been.

The emotional storm that had been gathering within him was apparently about to strike somewhere in some way. He took slow, deep breaths, made his way to the sink where he doused his face with cool water, dried himself and then examined his reflection in the mirror. Who was he and why was this happening to him?

"See anything interesting in there, fella?"

Paul spun around, stunned and looked into the face of a senior citizen wearing what looked like a farmer's attire, even down to the grimy work boots caked with dried mud. His face was round, red and jovial and it invited conversation. His pale blue eyes twinkled in the light above the mirror. The two of them were alone. Alone in the wash room.

"What?"

"I say, do you see anything interesting in that, there mirror?"

Paul smiled. "Nah, same ol', same ol'."

"Ain't it the truth."

He waved the mirror off with a gnarled hand.

"Too much water under the bridge and too many miles on this here carcass to be worryin' 'bout bein' 'ready for my close-up, Mr. De Mille.'"

Paul laughed at that one.

"Yeah, done a bunch o' jobs over the years; each one done give me another o' these here wrinkles! Been a barber here for the last little while. I kindly like it; ya gits to know people whiles they's a-sittin' in the chair and yer workin' on their noggins for 'em."

For some reason, the stranger's demeanor was acting like a psychic zipper. Paul feared he would be emotionally exposed in another minute. And it was as though he had no control over his psychological self at all.

"You look a little off kilter, son. Everythin' all right?"

"You know, it's funny you should ask that, but, no; I guess I haven't been 'all right' for a long time now."

The old fellow crossed his arms over his chest and leaned back against the stall wall behind him, adjacent to the sinks.

He nodded. "Go on, then."

With arched brows Paul asked, "Seriously?"

"As the proverbial heart attack."

The man's smile was infectious.

Paul turned toward the window, the one open just enough to let the outside air in.

"I had a best friend in high school. Oh, I guess I'm going back about twenty-five years or so."

The man thrust his chin out slightly as if he were considering the tale Paul was beginning to spin for possible publication.

"We drifted apart the last year of school. I felt bad about that; I really did. But neither of us ever really did anything about the situation. I remember being out for a walk one night about a block from his house. I looked up and saw his bedroom light on. I knew he was in there, probably reading a comic book or something. Anyway, I stood there for what seemed like the longest few minutes in recorded history. Just stood there, half of me wanting to run over there and make things right and the other half fearing rejection or worse."

The man coughed. "And you decided against going."

Paul sighed. "I did."

"Ever try later, after graduation, after you started off on your journey through life?"

Paul's eyes began to glisten slightly.

"I couldn't."

The old gentleman squinted in Paul's direction.

"He died. My best friend died," Paul offered.

The old man shook his head from side to side.

"Now that there's a toughy. Losin' a friend to an early death. Why, mine died in four foot o' water 'n' he was a swimmer. Nah, ya never do get over one o' those too easy-like."

Paul interrupted. "Thing is, they called it a suicide. But Larry, that was his name, Larry wasn't the type of kid to do something like that. He just wasn't."

The senior citizen put his hands on his hips in a posture of deliberation.

"Suicide, eh? Now that there is yer bitter pill, ain't she?"

"You know, lately it's been coming back to me: a lot. Maybe it's because I just got the newsletter from our high school about our twenty-fifth reunion, I don't know, but I can't seem to shake the idea that there was some kind of foul play involved in Larry's death."

"*Po*-lice looked into it, I reckon?"

"Yeah, but nothing solid ever came up. There had been talk for years about cases of molestation, though. Some stories about the parish priests, others about janitors and cleanup crews."

"And?" he offered, the twinkle still in his eyes.

"'And,' lately I find myself wondering if maybe something like that had happened to Larry. You know, some kind of abuse he just couldn't live with any longer. Not that he didn't take his life: maybe he did. But *why* he did. I just wonder if there wasn't something I could have done to prevent it. Maybe if I'd gone over to his house that night, I could have helped him. Lately, I've even considered trying to have his case reopened by the authorities."

The old man placed a firm and reassuring hand on Paul's shoulder.

"Listen here now, son. He was your friend: your best friend. Remember him that way. This thing you're troublin' yourself about, it's bein' takin' care of. Leave him with God and time. Time heals in magical ways you and I can never understand. Just leave it alone. Trust me, it's bein' taken care of."

A wave of relief washed over Paul replacing the darkness of the previous few months. And all because of a few words from a wise old stranger during a chance meeting in a restaurant rest room.

The relief was short-lived.

He looked down at his middle now. The searing pain was

keeping pace with the ever-widening blotch of rich, red blood filling his shirt like the opening of an umbrella.

The razor blade exited as quickly and deftly as it had entered.

Paul fell against the tile wall between the sinks, slid down into a sitting position, close to the floor, the lemony-smelling floor that reminded him of high school and a tragedy his tender conscience wouldn't allow him to forget.

He was watching the crusty boots now as they made their way away from him, the stranger speaking to him over his shoulder as he approached the door.

"Was a barber the last little while, all right...and a high school janitor before that."

COFFEE SHOP

It seemed like it was getting more and more difficult to get out of the little black roadster. But it only had twenty nine thousand miles on it and he was able to talk the owner down to ninety five hundred dollars. Not a bad price for a fourth mid-life crisis. It was certainly cheaper than funding another failed relationship.

The metal on the door was cold to his fingers as he slammed it shut. The coffee shop's neon *Open* sign welcomed him again and already the thought of Monday morning wasn't so over-powering after all. In a few minutes he'd be alone with a hot drink and a good book. Work could wait, at least for another half hour.

He hadn't planned to spend the beginning of his day trying to keep from staring over his café mocha at a tall, statuesque blonde. It had sneaked up on him, like those memories from years past that bob to the surface of consciousness as you transition from sleep to awareness.

He was minding his own business sharing the hot comfort drink with Ray Bradbury (a very unusual book of short stories at that) when the bell over the door tinkled and two ladies in their early twenties burst in, cackling about a wedding reception. The first was shorter, blonder and heavier. The second was, well, breathtaking. He would never forget her face because she looked directly into his eyes from the doorway to his table, the last one in the small shop. And smiled.

Eyes the color of a fading afternoon sky sparked recognition in him. He returned her smile before his conscience could object and then quickly resumed his story. But only for a moment. Then he returned to her, studying her, classifying her and trying to remember where he had seen her. The two young girls were ordering now; their voices broke his reverie and he told himself to concentrate on his story. He couldn't: with apologies to Mr. Bradbury.

Patty.

She was anything but spectacularly dressed. Faded jeans, a beige sweater and floppy jacket did nothing to display her as she ought to have been displayed. He could imagine her on a pedestal doing rhythmic, quarter turns inside a plastic bubble placed on a mantel. Shake it and snow would alight on her eyebrows, cheeks and shoulders. And that's when it came to him.

Patty.

She looked for all the world like his high school crush from a million years ago. He remembered how his friend had "spied out the land," and then given him the go ahead to ask her to the sophomore semi-formal. It had been all he had dreamed of in those late night musings in his bedroom as he looked out the window, past the telephone wires into the night sky, the street-lights glowing tiredly in the darkness.

The dance.

His friend had talked his older brother, the one with the polio limp, into lending him his GTO, a fiery red chariot with more than enough horses to speed the four of them on their way to adolescent euphoria. And it had been just that. It was a scene from a movie, that last dance of the evening when the music stopped and the dancing continued, he and Patty, gliding around in circles, the rest of the class standing, mutely watching a milestone moment in two young lives. He recalled the awkward silence as the two of them smiled into each other's eyes and reluctantly shuffled back to their table to gather sweater and jacket and purse.

* * * * * * *

The two girls were seated now, the one with glasses facing him, the other with back turned but with head tilted occasionally, ever so slightly, to her right and behind her.

Was she aware of him?

What was it? A reminder? Of days long ago, of a broken promise?

* * * * * * *

There had been the New Year's Eve party. And he had been invited. And Patty would be there, for *him*, Steve had said. And he should go. Of course, he should go. But he didn't. Another invitation had been accepted. From another girl, two years younger than he. They didn't *date*; not exactly. They were neither boyfriend and girlfriend nor *just* friends. Their relationship was simply their attempt at the meeting of emotional needs through the nearest physical equivalent. It wasn't sexual but physical, as if enough hugging and kissing and petting could somehow salve the inner wounds of abuse in their hearts placed there by parents and siblings and classmates.

"My parents won't be home on New Year's Eve," Ellen had said.

"Billy can be with Sue and you can be with me. We'll listen to music and lie in the darkness by the Christmas tree with only the tree lights shining. It'll be wonderful," she'd said. And in its own way it was.

* * * * * * *

But that night was twenty-five years and three failed marriages ago. He'd found out later that no one was at the party for Patty after all. She had been expecting *him*.

A few days later he had stopped by her home to apologize. She looked up from her cookie baking, flour on her faded jeans and beige sweater, tan hands and freckled face. She feigned anger with a wry smile, but revealed something else, too, in those pale, blue eyes.

Disappointment.

And he wondered about *her* late night reveries, *her* teenage dreams of Prince Charming as she gazed at her reflection in her vanity mirror. Had he really been offered emotional salvation so long ago through a blonde-headed soul mate's invitation to a New Year's Eve party he had not attended? He would never know.

* * * * * * *

His cup was empty now and he brushed the bagel crumbs from his jacket, closed the paperback and pocketed his cellular phone.

"Patty must be about like me, over forty or so by now," he mused to himself.

He fished some dollar bills out of his pocket, paid for his breakfast and quickly passed the table where the two young women were still discussing the upcoming wedding preparations. He wouldn't look at her. He couldn't.

Just then, another young girl approached the door as he opened it. She smiled as he held it open for her, the cool air chilling him. Heard her greet the other two young women at the table as he left and made his way to his car.

"You guys are early," he heard her say.

And then she added, "Hi Patty."

NUMBER EIGHT

"Palmer's" was one of a kind: unique.

There were greasy spoons and fast food joints, there were fancy eating establishments by the street full.

But only one Palmer's.

Food could be gotten anywhere; Palmer's offered...atmosphere. Enter here and be anyone you desire. Tucked away in the first floor of a downtown skyscraper it was more than a coffee shop. It was a magic carpet. Sit at the counter and travel anywhere in the world for as little as the price of "Number eight" on the menu: corned beef hash, complete with two poached eggs, toast, juice and coffee.

Palmer's.

"Through these doors march the varied flavors and textures of American humanity," it seemed to say. "This is the place! Problems solved here, fences mended, relationships restored, new hope dispatched to discouraged hearts with every refilled coffee cup. Try us once and try us twice; here you'll find everything's nice."

But could he count on it today?

Would the magic work today? Now, with this?

He stood in the doorway, glanced around, caught the manager's eye. She was a pert forty five, well-proportioned and personable. She always looked the same. She could have moonlighted as a mannequin in the store window next door in the arcade.

Smiling, she motioned him to a booth at the back of the room. He strode past the lunch crowd which was jammed into every seat and booth in the place. The air was crowded with cigarette smoke and the aroma of coffee and bacon. Self-consciously, he slid into the black, vinyl seat, his shoulder pressing against the mirrored wall. He tapped his fingers on the table, snatched the menu from the metal clip, packets of sugar tumbling out of their container. He stuffed them back in and flipped the menu open and then over. "Breakfast Specials" greeted his eyes.

"Why even bother looking?" he mused to himself. Redheaded Agnes approached him, reading his thoughts aloud with a smile on her too-thickly colored mouth.

"Number eight, Mr. Simpson?"

"Why Agnes, you're psychic," he laughed. "Thanks, Hon, and don't forget...."

"Whole wheat toast," she interrupted with a wink.

He dropped his chin into his right palm, his elbow leaning on the table, and watched the old girl waddle into the kitchen. He mused about the men whom had seen a younger version of that gait forty years ago, seen it, and tried to muster up enough nerve to ask her out on a date.

"I'll bet you were a real, 'razzamatazz,' Aggie," he said to himself. He smiled. "A real catch."

A few minutes later she returned and poured the hot, black energizer into the white, porcelain cup. He lifted the paper juice container to his lips and tried to pour orange juice onto the tickly coldness in his stomach. Refusing to drown, the feeling intensified. He added milk and sugar to his coffee and sipped slowly, nonchalantly, presenting a confidence he didn't possess. He glanced at his watch. "Maybe she won't show," he thought.

Just then, the scent of perfume filled his nostrils; his toes actually tingled. He had been so lost in thought and nerves that he hadn't seen her approach. She stood at the table, clad in a dark blue trench coat.

He half-stood, motioned her to join him, fumbled, took her coat and hung it on the wall rack while she adjusted her sweater, looking out of the corner of her eye into the mirror to her left.

With his back to her, he wished that the clothes peg were a

trigger to a secret compartment, that he could pull it and vanish behind to some dark, forgotten chamber.

He turned and took his seat opposite her, looked into her pale, blue eyes.

She was absolutely gorgeous. No exaggeration. He had noticed office workers actually staring as she walked past. At five-foot six, one hundred twenty five pounds, with snow-white hair and a porcelain complexion, she was almost too beautiful to touch or talk to. As if too close a contact with "reality" might shatter her into a million pieces.

"Sorry I'm late," she whispered, a smile filling her face.

"Gosh, it's good to be in here; getting cold outside," she said as she rubbed the outsides of her arms.

"Yeah," he mumbled. "It is getting chilly; guess November's gonna be a bear."

She cocked her head to one side and stared, silent. He felt disarmed by her gaze.

"Uh, what did you want...breakfast...lunch?" He asked.

"Whatever you're having," she smiled.

"Number eight," said Agnes as she reappeared, positioning the food in front of him. "Now what can I get for you, Honey?"

"Number eight it is," Julie replied, nodding her head with a sense of triumph as she took her seat opposite him.

"Whole wheat toast?" asked the waitress.

"Sure, why not?" Julie replied, tossing her head, her hair spilling over her shoulders. She placed her chin in her palms and rested her elbows on the table looking straight into his eyes, through them, down to the tingly feeling deep within him.

"Well, what's the verdict? Did you tell her?"

He glanced down, played with the napkin in his lap.

"Julie," he stammered. His mouth was dry, his tongue was thick, his saliva was glue.

"Adam, you mean you didn't tell her? You didn't say anything, no explanation, no apology...nothing?"

She turned from him and looked vacantly out the window. Disgust pursed her lips.

Adam sighed. He looked at the plate in front of him, toyed with the hash, jabbed at the egg in the center, wondering if he would ever be hungry again.

"Julie, that weekend was...was like heaven. It really was; you've got to believe me. Everything I said, it was true, all of it; I swear it was."

He tried with everything within him to reassure this girl, nearly half his age, that he hadn't "used her," really hadn't. He yearned to convince her that that weekend had been the happiest of his life. His words weren't working.

Her gaze turned to his. Their eyes were riveted together. Her disdain dissipated; it had only been fleeting anyway. She surprised herself at the feeling that took its place. She labeled it in an instant: relief. It was the honest-to-goodness kind of grade school relief she'd felt when the bell rang just as she was about to read her report aloud to the class. The emotion embarrassed her. She tried to at least appear inquisitive.

Agnes rescued her with the arrival of "Number eight."

"Can I get you two anything else?" she asked in textbook waitress-speak.

"No; this will be fine," Tom assured her with a weak smile.

How did a thirty five year old accountant, married for twelve years, with two kids, just pick up and agree to meet a high school graduate—a summer assistant—in New York, a thousand miles away, for a weekend? What in the world had been so special about picking her up at the airport, spending six meals with her? He hadn't slept with her; they hadn't even kissed.

Those meals, a trip to the museum and a concert had somehow bundled up fifteen years of mediocrity and tossed it out of his life, forever.

He was a changed person. About the only thing they had done was talk, really talk. That was something he and Sally had stopped doing a million years ago.

He remembered thinking about all those clichés concerning "quality time" and "real communication" on the plane, with his forehead pressed against the cool window pane. Julie hadn't occupied his thoughts during that night flight: Sally had. Their entire relationship had sped before his mind's eye like a video at high speed. He loved her.

Julie ate her breakfast, dutifully, methodically. Her heart raced at the thought of "dating around." She cared for Adam, really cared; he made her feel safe, accepted, desired. But in her heart she remembered how the "electricity" had waned after he'd hugged her as she came down from the ramp at the airport. She winced as she recalled the hollow feeling that remained with her as she took the early flight back from New York. Something seemed missing. Maybe it was ten years of dates and dreams and experiences she would be denied by giving herself to this older, sadder man.

She looked up from her food with a tiny tear in the corner of her eye. Slowly, she reached her hand across the table and placed it gently over his.

"That weekend *was* wonderful," Julie whispered.

He grasped the understanding she offered behind those words, grasped it and scooped it up like a miner sifting sand for gold. He treasured it and took it to his heart.

Relieved, he sighed and wiped a tear from his own eye.

"Julie...," he offered.

She pressed a slender finger to his lips.

"Don't."

They held each other's hands across the table until Agnes brought the check.

THE TYPEWRITER

The cardboard hurt his fingers as he ripped open the carton. He fumbled the machine out of its box. His heartbeat quickened as the weight of the typewriter landed on his study desk. He sighed and plopped down on the metal chair. He smiled, contented.

He looked down at the keyboard with glee: childlike glee. At last he could be a "writer!" Who could write a decent article, let alone a short story or novel without a "real" typewriter...like this one: electronic, with automatic centering, bold-faced type and right margin justification? But now he had it; he had it all. Time, talent...and the typewriter!

He looked up from this gray plastic and metal servant and gazed absentmindedly out the window at the leafy, green trees in the backyard. After a few seconds, his attention jerked back to the machine waiting in front of him: silent, innocent, guileless.

He must begin!

He actually slapped his hands together, rubbing them briskly before his fingers found the appropriate keys.

"Oh, the plug, of course," he thought. "It's electronic, not like the ones in high school. Not like those damaged ancient ones he'd used in college. This was a real piece of work: a modern, metal miracle of the '80s! Why, it claimed to do everything for you but make breakfast. To believe the brochure, it almost thought."

A slight whirring sound lifted the curtain on his initial

performance. He pressed the "justification" mode and stared expectantly at the display. He would actually see the words he'd type before they would appear on the paper. Would he ever need the correction ribbon? He knew the inventor must have been a genius.

"What do I write?" he asked himself, there in the afternoon-quiet of his study. "An essay, an article, a short story...the world's greatest novel?"

"Better start small," he answered himself. "Don't overwhelm the reader all at once. There's a whole lifetime of creativity and unplumbed talent just waiting to be tapped. Why shoot the works right off the bat?"

"Speaking of shooting, do you own a gun?"

The clickety-click of the keys was followed by absolute silence. The kind that made house noises and car metal creaking audible. Perspiration sprang from the pores on his forehead and back. He looked down slowly at his pudgy fingers, as though afraid of being caught.

They hadn't moved.

He took a deep breath and scooped the instruction manual up into the light of the lamp directly over his desk.

"I bet somebody goofed this thing up," he sighed to himself, disgusted.

If patience was a virtue, impatience was his vice. Irritability, actually: at everyone and everything. His car was a moving courtroom and he was judge, jury and executioner; court was in session during every rush hour.

He scanned the manual in vain for anything about a "demon-stration mode."

But there it was: a sentence he hadn't written. It stared at him: crisp, black ink on cool, white paper.

"What the hell?" he mused, exasperated. "What's this supposed to signify, 'Do you own a gun'?"

The sentence remained, unimpressed at either his incredulity or his mounting anger. It was "high noon" at six o'clock in the third floor of a small, old house in suburban Washington, D.C.

And he was unarmed.

"Maybe strangling would be more satisfying."

Again, the keys moved automatically, the spelling and punctuation, perfect.

"Strangling!" he exclaimed to himself.

The back of his shirt was a drenched dish rag. He leaned forward from the chair back, straining to free himself from the suction created by his sweat. His flabby stomach creased over the desk as he again looked out the window at the quarter-acre, grassy lot below.

"This thing's talking to me."

He looked at the paper, anticipating the next remark.

The carriage moved as if on cue.

"What do you want to do, divorce her?"

"What *do* you do to an unfaithful wife?"

"I'd kill her," the machine answered itself, nonchalantly.

"Kill her?" he asked it, out loud this time.

"Suit yourself. We're all different. You have to live with yourself; she's your wife. *I'd* kill her."

The room was absolutely still.

He leaned forward, peering over the paper guide like a child creeping up on a bird.

The carriage flew away from his gaze.

"*Do* you own a gun?"

He slumped back in his chair, terrified, his clammy hands covering his face.

"What's going on?" he asked himself in the quiet of the evening.

The air was mute.

The machine was silent.

He was alone with his thoughts.

He slid away from the small computer chair and into the rocker. He spun in the direction of the window and stared at the huge oak tree in the distance. His eyes remained there while his thoughts traveled swiftly, spanning the past six months. The memories were a menagerie of stress. He was overweight, his blood pressure had finally climbed from "borderline" to "high." His smoking had doubled to keep pace with his drinking. And Pat? She was getting a new lease on life with the health foods, the civic club meetings and that damned aerobics class. Why the hell did they use male instructors anyway? It was ridiculous and "No, he didn't want to join in," thank you very much.

He closed his eyes and let the weight of his head sink back into the chair cushion. He stretched his feet out in front of him, sprawling there like a beached fish.

"Who needs any of it?" he thought.

The job was just a means to an end, a way to pay the bills until his writing paid off. All he needed was a decent type-writer. That's all; every artist needs adequate supplies. In a little while he could "kiss the job"...and Pat. To hell with herbs and the Joneses and diets and running in circles trying to look like a teenager. Writers were supposed to drink and smoke and over-indulge with food.

He guessed she'd been seeing the instructor for at least a month. It had been that long since she'd last mentioned his weight. She had stopped inviting him to the club meetings. She'd also stopped cooking dinner, especially on Fridays. And he knew there was no class on Fridays. And he hated him; oh, how he hated that slimy, spindly, energetic twit. People with that kind of self-discipline should be shot on principle.

"She's with him now, you know. It's Friday. The day's over and there's no supper cooking and she didn't leave a note. You're here with me and she's away with him."

His pulse quickened, his vision blurred, as he jumped up and glared at the page, watching each new word being fastened to the paper by twentieth-century precision.

"Forget...about...her;...I'll kill...himmmm...," he slurred as he brought his fist down on the keyboard.

The room spun and the trees merged into one mass of foliage as he sank to the floor. They seemed to be brooding over him as he lost consciousness for the last time.

Then the room was quiet, except for a faint whirring.

Borgo Press Books by JACK HALLIDAY

Kawanga: A Mystery Novel
Swan Song and Other Mystery Stories

SWAN SONG AND OTHER MYSTERY STORIES

Screenwriter Chip Delaney just wants to cure his writer's block with an impromptu drive to a small town a few hours from LA. But his vehicle is smashed within minutes of his arrival, and then he's pummeled in his room atop the unusual town's only diner. Gradually he becomes involved with Audrey, owner of the truck stop. As his relationship develops, he begins receiving strange phone calls, random rifle shots, and cryptic cell phone texts. This poignant and moving noir novella will stun you with, not one, but *two* satisfying twist endings that would have made Mickey Spillane proud!

The stories that follow range from dark, hardboiled fare like "Moonlight and Roses" and "Washroom Talk," to crime tales such as "Black Sunrise" and "Stalking Susan Storm," to poignant, "slice-of-life" relationship pieces like "Number Eight" and "Coffee Shop," and even a fantasy story. Now: sit back, relax, and enjoy the ride! Jack Halliday is a major new talent!

www.ingramcontent.com/pod-product-compliance
Lightning Source LLC
Chambersburg PA
CBHW020320260626
47156CB00004B/1300